VOL. 2, NO. 1 ISSUE 31

Fiction

Chivaine, by John R. Fultz 4
Give Me the Daggers, by Adrian Cole 14
The Music of Bleak Entrainment, by Gary A. Braunbeck 34
Into The Mountains with Mother Old Growth, by Christian Riley . . 45
The Grimlorn Under the Mountain, by James Aquilone 58
Dolls, by Paul Dale Anderson 69
Gut Punch, by Jason A. Wyckoff 83
Educational Upgrade, by Bret McCormick 97
Boxes of Dead Children, by Darrell Schweitzer 111
The Forgotten, by D.C. Lozar 120
Coffee with Dad's Ghost, Jessica Amanda Salmonson 124
Missed It By That Much, by Gregg Chamberlain 125
A Clockwork Muse, by Erica Ruppert 127
The Rookery, by Kurt Newton 132
Wolf of Hunger, Wolf of Shame, by J. T. Glover 134
Zucchini Season, by Janet Harriett 141
The Jewels That Were Their Eyes, by Llanwyre Laish 143
The Twins, by Kevin Strange 152
Princess or Warrior?, by S.W. Lauden 157

Poetry

The City in the Sands, by Ann K. Schwader 13
NecRomance, by Frederick J. Mayer 32
Walpurgis Eve, K.A. Opperman 44
Sonnets of an Eldritch Bent, W. H. Pugmire 56
Castle Csejthe, Ashley Dioses 96
The Shrine, Wade German 131
Bride of Death, by Dave Reeder 137
Modern Primitive, by Chad Hensley 140

Staff

Publisher and Executive Editor: *John Gregory Betancourt*
Consulting Editor: *W. Paul Ganley*
Editor: *Doug Draa*
Production Manager: *Steve Coupe*

A Note from the Consulting Editor

Ever since Doug Draa told me his plans to revive *Weirdbook* I have been more or less speechless—and now they say I have to make a speech!—or at least write one. What can I say? I was totally amazed then and I continue to be totally amazed. I recall the state of fantasy/horror back in 1967 when I decided to start *Weirdbook*...hardly much being published at all, outside of the *Magazine of Horror*, which used mostly reprints! I was lucky to get three excellent writers for the first issue (Brennan, Munn, Howard) and ended up writing most of the rest of the issue myself under pennames, and using some reprints from my old fanzine from the fifties...with almost no artwork at all! And mailing out 500 giveaways (to supposedly interested persons) was like dropping them in the ocean tied to a ton of lead. Everything started very slowly. This is a new era...and I am extremely glad to see what a fine lineup we have for issue #31...writers and artists to be proud of! Great work, Doug!

—W. Paul Ganley

A Note from the Editor

We pulled it off.

You're holding the first issue of *Weirdbook* to appear since 1997!

Trying to live up to Paul Ganley's original World Fantasy Award winning magazine has been a daunting task, but I think that Paul will be satisfied with the selection of stories being offered here. I've made a point of staying true to the spirit of the magazine's original incarnation while simultaneously bringing it up into the 21st Century.

One of my major criteria for being accepting stories into *Weirdbook* is that they satisfy.

This is a reader's magazine and not a critic's. I honestly hope these stories meet with your approval and pleasure. You'll be running into established pros like Gary A. Braunbeck, Jessica Amanda Salmonson, Paul Dale Anderson, Adrian Cole and Ann K. Schwader. Other stories for your enjoyment are by rising stars such as John R. Fultz and James Aquilone. And backing this all up of is a slew of talented new writers who round out this premier relaunch issue.

I wish to thank everyone who has supported this project from the get go. I especially want to thank the following folks. Paul Ganley for allowing me to revive his child, John Betancourt for taking the chance on publishing *Weirdbook*, all of the wonderful writers who submitted more than 500 stories for consideration.

And lastly, I'd like to thank the readers who have invested their hard earned money so that they may read this collection of the weird and wonderful.

I thank each and everyone of you from the bottom of my heart!

Now get reading and make sure to tell your friends.

—Doug Draa

A Note from the Publisher

Being asked to take over as publisher of *Weirdbook* came as a surprise to me. But it was one I enjoyed, and one I'm happy to embrace. As the former publisher of *Weird Tales*, I certainly understand the challenges faced by weird fiction magazines, and hopefully I can start the new incarnation of *Weirdbook* on the road to success. I can't promise to be at the helm more than a couple of issues, but hopefully that will be enough to get it well launched for a prolonged new life under editor Doug Draa.

—John Betancourt

Chivaine

by John R. Fultz

"Chivaine!" they cried.

"Chivaine will return to us and all of this suffering will end."

Chivaine with his silver sword and gleaming mail. Chivaine with his lion eyes and quick limbs. Chivaine on his white horse strung with chains of gold and jewels.

Chivaine. Bane of Invaders.

Across the Land of Willows he was little more than a fable, a dream kept alive by frightened townsfolk gathered around their burning homes. The war was over and the land had been won not by its valiant defenders, but by the enemy. The horse tribes of the tundra had descended on the Land of Willows for the fifth time in as many generations. This time they had conquered all.

"Chivaine…" cried the witch on the mountain. She sprinkled bone dust over her fire and looked across the valley where the river flowed toward the Yellow Plain. Seven villages she counted burning in the valley. She rattled feathers and bones, spilled blood from her wrist to pacify the Demon of the Winds.

Forty years ago it had been Chivaine who led the Bright King's army to the field of Eleanim. Chivaine who led the king's men to victory, and Chivaine whose blade took the head of the Horselord Ugtuk Wolfstooth. Yet Chivaine had wandered into mystery during the decades of peace that followed his victory.

"Chivaine…" cried the witch. She called on the spirits of her ancestors, all those who had lived and died in the Land of Willows since the beginning of time. She spoke the names of dreadful powers known only to witches.

On this day the Land of Willows belonged to Barain Hawkheart, Lord of Horses, heir to the Druid Crown. Slayer of the Bright King. With fear and fire and iron blades his raiders came south on the backs of stallions bred for war. The Willow Folk were unprepared, used to peaceful living, forgetful of their hard-fought past victories. They were easily conquered.

Yet they remembered Chivaine. As the Bright King's citadel fell and the northmen torched entire towns, the Willow Folk remembered the Hero of Eleanim.

"Chivaine will return," they said. "Chivaine will bring us freedom."

The conquerors walked the streets and orchards claiming whatever they wanted. They violated women and temples, slaying wildly in the name of Hawkheart. Packs of mounted raiders owned the roads. The Dreaming River ran red and corpses floated among the reeds. The Land of Willows burned, and Chivaine remained a dream.

"Chivaine!" said the witch. "He will be our vengeance. Come, Chivaine, hear the call of your people! Come to us now in the hour of our need."

A storm blew over the valley. Thunder roared *Chivaine!* and lightning struck the wooded slopes. The witch chanted and danced in the rain. Her fire smoldered but did not extinguish. As the storm faded, a dense fog crept into the valley and up its slopes.

The witch inhaled smoke from the embers and sat quietly in the fog. Listening. She listened with the patience of a stone until she heard a horse's hooves on gravel. A dark shape, a rider, moved through the mist. He came *down* the slope, as if from the mountain's unseen peak, and paused at the witch's camp. She stared at his face and raised her bony arms.

"Chivaine?" she sighed.

The man on the white horse was very old. His flesh sagged on his bones, as did the rusted mail on his shoulders and arms. Arms once big 'round as treetrunks, the stories said. His beard was white with streaks of grey. His eyes in their beds of wrinkles squinted at the witch and sparkled with mystery. A silver sword hung across his back.

"What is this place grandmother?" asked the knight.

"The Valley of the Dreaming River," said the witch. "Are you Chivaine?"

The old man blinked and rubbed his beard. He wore steel gauntlets as rusted as his armor.

"That might have been my name," he said.

"What were you?" she asked, waving a crow feather at him.

The knight looked into the fog, or into the depths of his foggy memories.

"I was a hero," he said.

"Then be so again," said the witch. She rose, dubbed his forehead and shoulders with a blackthorn branch, as a queen blessing her champion. The knight offered her a kindly smile, but shook his head.

"I am too old," he said. "Too tired. I wish only to rest."

The toothless witch grinned, a horrible sight for anyone to see.

"I have called you from the Deadlands," she said. "You may not return to your well-deserved rest until the man called Hawkheart is driven from our land."

The knight bowed his head. He seemed to have fallen asleep.

"You are Chivaine!" she said, shaking him awake. "You are the Bright King's blade! Bane of Invaders! Go now and bid your people to rise up and slay their oppressors! Go take the head of Barain Hawkheart as you took that of Ugtuk Wolfstooth. Bring it here to me if you would regain your eternal rest."

"I am Chivaine," said the knight. "Yet I am not the same Chivaine who felled the Wolfstooth. I was younger and stronger then. Foolish enough to be courageous. Convinced of my own invincibility. I would learn eventually that all these headstrong truths were lies. Untruths that I told to make myself strong. Lies I told the world."

"If lies are strength, then find that strength again," said the witch. He could not refuse the power of her geas. "Go!"

The white horse sped down the slope and Chivaine inhaled the sweet honey of the mountain air. Mammoth lillies were in blossom this time of year. He galloped through a field of tall, drooping flowers that bobbed and nodded like praying monks.

Riding along the riverside he smelled the reek of the burning villages. He saw blood and bodies floating on the river. He stopped, slid from his saddle, and walked to the water. Found an unspoiled place to drink.

His own starlit face looked back at him from the water's surface. His beard was darker now, his face less wrinkled. He was not so old as he had imagined. The water was cool, bringing strength to his limbs. His broad shoulders filled the rusted mail better than they had at the witch's camp.

"Chivaine…"

A voice called to him from beneath the water. Several voices, all repeating his name.

"Spirits of the dead," he said. "I hear you."

"Avenge us, Chivaine," said the voices. "Bring us the head of the Hawkheart."

"That prize I have already promised to a lady on the mountain," said Chivaine. "But I will give you a taste of this tyrant's blood, once I have cut him down."

The water spirits cooed and bubbled. "Take with you the power of our own blood flowing in this river, that it might not be lost entirely."

Chivaine climbed into his saddle. A forgotten vitality sang in his arms and legs. It churned in his chest like a battle cry ready to be set free.

The hooves of his white horse beat against the earth as he flew between the flaming husks of farms and hamlets. Following the trail of bodies and wreckage he came to the valley's end, where the land spread itself flat and the river flowed toward the great plain.

There Chivaine found the great encampment of Barain Hawkheart. The northmen were enjoying the rewards of plundering and pillaging. They had claimed this land, and now they claimed its spoils. Ale, meat, and captive women flowed between their tents of elk hide. The screams of victims mingled with the slow cadence of drunken war chants sung about the fires. Thousands of fine northern horses were picketed in haphazard rows about the site. The despoilers of the valley thought all their enemies dead or in hiding, so they celebrated and forgot their native caution.

Chivaine rode into the mass of carousing northmen swift as an arctic wind. His blade cut a red path toward Hawkheart's pavilion. The blood of northmen rained upon his ancient mail, somehow cleansing it of rust and filth. His armor gleamed as bright as his silver blade. His beard was black as midnight, his face young and defiant. He grinned at the red carnage about him, exulting in the slaughter.

"I am Chivaine!" he roared. "Bane of Invaders! From beyond death I have come to take the life of the Hawkheart..."

At last the crowds of panicked raiders spread apart, revealing their champion, the reaver who had delivered their greatest victory, Barain Hawkheart himself. His chain mail was black with soot, his war helm set with a crown of jagged spikes. His mount was a dark behemoth of horseflesh with iron-shod hooves, trained to split the skulls of footsoldiers.

Hawkheart peered through his visor at the hero of southern legend. He knew the fables like everyone else. He understood this Chivaine was a specter from the netherworld, but he did not care. He was the Lord of Horses, ordained by his savage gods to spread conquest. The entire world was his to take as he had taken the Land of Willows. No man, dead or alive, would stop his colossal ambition.

"Shade!" Hawkheart hailed Chivaine. "Revenant!" He raised a great axe in each hand. "You have forgotten the sweet embrace of death. So come. Lct me refresh your memory."

The two horses and their riders collided. Sparks flew from scraping metal, drops of blood fell to the muddy earth. The riders swirled like battling storms striking thunderbolts at one another. The northmen gathered in a great circle about the combat, cheering their hero, spitting and cursing Chivaine's name.

"If you kill me I will only return to the Deadlands," Chivaine said. "And if I kill you that same return is my promised reward."

"Then why not let me slay you?" said Hawkheart. "I'll send you back to the dead country quickly and painlessly."

"Look at the red river," said Chivaine. He struck and parried, his greatsword leaping between the two great axes. "Look at the burning villages. See the bodies of the dead trampled into the earth, hear the wailing of war orphans. For all of these things you are damned. For these crimes I will send you to the Deadlands well before I return there."

Hawkheart grinned like a hyena. "I will wait for you on the other side of death. I'll give you no peace, even in the afterlife. Once I am dead too, you'll not be able to kill me again. We will fight this battle forever at the gates of the Deadlands."

Chivaine answered with the thrust of his blade through his opponent's neck. The sword sliced open Hawkheart's jugular. Blood gushed to drown his blackened breastplate. He dropped his axes, raised hands to his spurting neck.

"This is your choice," Hawkheart said. His voice rasped and he coughed blood."You'll find no more rest in death… Only me waiting for you…"

"I am Chivaine," said the knight. He swept the silver blade sideways and finished beheading the Lord of Horses. Hawkheart's head fell into the muck and rolled a short way, its eyes still blinking through the visor. His body fell from the black horse and lay still upon the red earth.

"Now we are both legends," said the head. Its eyes grew still.

Chivaine's horse and mail gleamed crimson. He spun about, bent to grab up Hawkheart's head, and rode back the way he had come. He trampled or cut down any outlanders foolish enough to get in his way.

The army of northmen wailed and fell into disorder. Without their warlord to calm tribal hatreds they fought among themselves. Several skirmishes broke out at the heart of the horde, while tribal bands along its edges rode into the night. Better to leave with whatever treasures were gained this season than to stay and lose everything. They had taken gold, women, and weapons of steel from the Land of Willows. Every warpath must come to an end and most of the northmen were ready to go home anyway. Hawkheart might have driven them eastward to plunder the cities of the Yellow Plain next. But Hawkheart was dead and so was his campaign of conquest.

Chivaine went back to the river as he had promised and sprinkled a few drops of Hawkheart's blood to appease the water spirits. Then he rode hard along the High West Road leading out of the valley into the heart of the Bright King's domain. Always bearing Hawkheart's head in his raised fist, he passed from one shattered town to another.

Commoners and noblefolk cheered him on together.

"Chivaine!" they called in the morning sun. "Chivaine has saved us!"

"Chivaine has killed the Horse Lord!"

Across the Land of Willows the knight rode and displayed his grisly trophy. Men took up spears and pitchforks and rusted blades, determined now to drive out the remaining invaders. The savages had no heart for a fight without a dominant force to unite them. History had show this again and again. The Bright King was dead, but Chivaine had returned.

"Chivaine!" they cried from town square and ruined tower, from the decks of riverboats and the slopes of mountain glens. "Chivaine lives!"

After nine days of ceaseless riding Chivaine returned to the witch on her mountain. Hawkheart's head was rotten and brimming with deathworms. Still the knight held it dangling by its long black hair. Summer rains had washed the crimson from Chivaine's mail. He gleamed sun-bright on the mountainside as he presented the witch her prize. She danced about the decaying head of Hawkheart and sang an ancient song. She placed it in a jar full of beetles that would eat away the putrid flesh and preserve the skull.

"You have done well, Chivaine," said the witch. "You have earned the pleasure of a fine drink before you embrace death again." She poured him a goblet of wine, an ancient vintage that had lain hidden in her cave for a lifetime. Except for the river water it was the only thing Chivaine had ingested since his return to the living realm. He savored its heady flavors on his tongue.

Chivaine took off his helm and admired the green valley. Sunrise gleamed bright on the river. The bodies had all been burned or buried. The blood had been washed away from the land as it had been washed from his armor. The Willow Folk were rebuilding along the riverbanks. Sailing boats brought provisions and laborers into the valley. Where the northern horde had camped there was now only a heap of charred bones, the remains of a communal pyre. The sun was golden with the heat of summer, the sky blue and brilliant.

"Time to resume your eternal rest," said the witch. "Return now to the Deadlands."

"I no longer wish to return," said Chivaine. "I want to stay." His young eyes gleamed.

"What?" said the witch. "Forsake your well-earned rest?"

"You've reminded me of life's splendors," said the knight.

"Not all of them," said the witch. She stepped in front of Chivaine and he saw her as a young and lovely maiden. "I know what it is you hunger for. I too remember that hunger." Her dark eyes glimmered and his heart fluttered beneath the silver curiass. She was very beautiful and the night sky gleamed in the folds of her black hair.

Chivaine walked close to her. "Are you in truth this comely girl?" he asked. "Or only a hag wearing a glamour?"

"Are you in truth a living man of flesh and blood?" she asked. "Or a dead spirit called forth to roam the physical world?"

Chivaine could not answer.

"It does not matter," she said. She kissed him. Hey lay with her in the cave where she kept her pots, talismans, and hanging herbs. All the splendor of the flesh that he had forgotten in death's numb grip, all the deep pleasure of sharing one's self with another, all of these things she gave him. Later they lay outside the cave and watched the stars winking at them.

"In nine months I will bear a son from this union," said the witch. "I will name him Chivaine."

The knight looked at her. "How can this be?" he asked. "Can the dead conceive the living?" Already her face seemed older, more worn. The magic of her glamour was fading.

"Death…life," she said. "Both are curtains, easily swept aside. Or kept in place to obscure the truth of where we all dwell."

"And where is that?" he said.

"Eternity," she said. Now she was old and wrinkled again, her hair a tangle of wispy gray.

"You cannot stay in this world," she said. "You belong in the Deadlands. By the power of our shared flesh I command you to return. Now."

Chivaine dressed himself in the silver mail and mounted his horse. Fog rolled down the mountain and he rode into it with a single backward glance. He glimpsed the maiden one last time. She waved at him as he disappeared from the living world. Then only the mountain witch stood before the cave. She wiped her swelling eyes and went in to sleep. Tomorrow she would begin to prepare the cave for the child to come.

Chivaine rode through the fog until the gray world of the Deadlands took shape before him. The ruins of toppled citadels and fallen cities lay spread across a dusty flatland. Phantoms danced and shivered in the air. The dead sky was silver and full of gleaming black stars. Ahead rose the Great Gate where dead souls pass into the afterlife.

A mighty figure stood before the gate. The shade of Barain Hawkheart raised its twin axes, glared at Chivaine from behind its horned visor.

"I told you I would meet you here," said Hawkheart. "Now we fight again. Forever."

"No," said Chivaine. "I am tired of fighting." He had grown old again. His armor and sword were rusted, his beard long and snowy.

There was no strength left in his limbs. He slid down off his horse and rested on a broken column.

Hawkheart's ghost stamped through the bone dust to overshadow him.

"Fight!" said Hawkheart. "You must! Or I will slay you with a single swipe of this axe."

Chivaine laughed. "You cannot slay me. I'm already dead. So are you. To fight here would be pointless."

"No!" bellowed the Lord of Horses. "We will fight again, and again, throughout eternity. Get up, southern man!" He raised the great axes above Chivaine's head.

Chivaine tossed his rusted sword at the conqueror's feet. "I have sampled more than my fair share of life's delights," he said. "But that is all over now. I only wish only to rest." He yawned and lay his head back against the broken marble.

"So be it," said Hawkheart. He swung the great axe in an even arc, lopping the old knight's head from his shoulders. Rusted chain links and blood spattered across the dust. Hawkheart lifted the head of Chivaine high in mockery of what the hero had done to him in the living world. He climbed upon Chivaine's steed and rode it through the gates into the Deadlands, shouting his victory.

Once beyond the gate Chivaine's head faded to wisps of vapor in Hawkheart's fist. The Horselord looked back, flexing his empty fingers, but the gate was lost in grey mist. A horde of demons crept about him, drawn by the echoes of his boasting. He slashed at them with both axes, but could not cut their flesh. They laughed and screeched like apes while his blades sang through phantom bodies. They tore the axes away, carried him in their claws kicking and screaming to a great pit, where the cries of damned souls rose on columns of smoke and flame. They chained him to the wall of the burning abyss and began the first of his endless tortures.

Chivaine's thoughts blew on the wind like lotus blossoms. He remembered the swipe of the great axe and nothing else. He heard the sighing of celestial currents that flow between worlds. The scattered thoughts gathered like moths about a tiny and insistent flame, a golden pinpoint sun in the barren void. A great calm settled over these tattered shreds of being. They grew warm and dull and mingled with dreamstuff, floating in a brine of absolute serenity. What was left of Chivaine, an infinitesimal spark maybe, settled into its new home. Slept there for nine months.

On a day of brightness and pain he came back to the world again. A midwife pulled the squawling infant from the witch's womb. The hag had lost far too much blood during the birthing. She lay dying with the pink newborn in her arms.

“Chivaine,” she told the midwife. “His name is Chivaine.”

“A hero’s name,” said the midwife. She stared at the baby’s round and gentle face. His eyes were blue and something of the lion gleamed deep inside them.

The witch nodded. “Take him, raise him with kindness,” she said. “He will grow tall and strong like his father. And when the raiders again come screaming from the north, as they always do, hungry for our blood and gold, he will be there to greet them. Everyone will know his name.” She kissed her son once on his hairless head and died.

The midwife took little Chivaine from the cave and carried him into the valley. Her people were planting spring crops in neat rows along the riverside. A warm breeze played in the tops of the willows. She brought the babe into her simple home, telling everyone his name as she passed

One evening while the baby slept in its crib, she found a greatsword lying before her fireplace. No one in the village admitted to leaving it there, and none could even afford such a weapon. Its scabbard was ancient leather set with jewels and golden inlays, the blade itself forged of purest silver.

She laid the sword across her knees and watched the baby dream. So peaceful, so full of blessed innocence. Alas, it was the way of the world: Peace never lasted.

Outside the cold north wind moaned, swearing vengeance against the Land of Willows.

She hid the silver blade in a hole beneath her cottage.

It would be there when Chivaine needed it. ▲

Dedicated to the memory of
Tanith Lee,
Sorceress Supreme

The City in the Sands

by Ann K. Schwader

Because they understood no gods but theirs,
& cut themselves adrift from history,
A pack of ragged jackals made their lair
Among half-buried ruins, unaware
They trespassed in the realm of mysteries.

No hand of man raised up the nameless stones
That formed this place. No human thought conceived
Its guardians—for we are not alone,
& never have been through the eons flown
Since void-spawned terrors taught our world to grieve.

The jackals with their ropes & hammers broke
Each image of those guardians to shards
& shattered shadows. "Heresy", they spoke
In undertones, unwilling to provoke
The twilight creeping softly. Falling hard.

They kindled watch-fires in the city streets,
Sustaining them on scavenged texts whose tongues
Were old before Irem... & yet no heat
Arose from so much burning to defeat
A depth of desert chill that bit & stung.

At last a bitter gust of wind arose
That sent a thousand shadows clawing high
In spectral vengeance as their victims froze,
Acknowledging in vain the shapes of those
Lost guardians now blotting out the sky.

Bereft of men & gods alike, these walls
Lie silent in the selfsame dawn that shone
On Sarnath & Mnar. Here too the call
Of history rang clearly over all
This shifting sand that whispers over bones.

Give Me the Daggers

by Adrian Cole

From the files of Nick Nightmare

I've never been one for carnivals, or circuses or any of that kind of stuff. I don't like those insane rides or the grasping carnie one-armed bandits, and you can keep the Human Crocodile and the Bearded Lady with a zillion tattoos. My world is stuffed with enough freaks and I'd rather spend my hard-earned filthy lucre on something educational, like a bunch of comics. So when I took the call on my mobile, I wasn't thinking about carnivals.

There was no mistaking the thundering tones of Rizzie Carter, the local Police Chief. I knew from his voice that he was even more agitated than normal. I could almost smell the sweat of deep unease down the phone.

"Nick," he bawled. "We got big problems. Weird. As weird as it gets, even for you." He always talked to me like I was on the NYPD payroll. Sure, I helped him out with the bizarre and twisted stuff—which is how I earned my Nick Nightmare sobriquet—but I wasn't under contract. However, there was no point telling him that. He gave me an address—the last place on earth any sane guy would want to visit—and told me he'd see me as soon as I could get over there.

* * * *

I took a cab through New York's canyons to the very edge of civilization, to a beat-up area that looked about due for flattening and redeveloping. It was more like a war zone, as if I'd somehow skipped across half the world into Beirut, or Iraq. Those buildings that hadn't collapsed looked like they'd be next and I half expected to hear gunfire. The cab pulled up short of the address Rizzie had given me and I saw a number of cops approaching us from a cordon. I paid the driver and he was glad to swing the cab round and hightail it out of there. For two cents I'd have gone with him.

I unzipped a wad of gum and chewed it. Looking around into the oncoming dusk, I felt like something dark and unsympathetic was eyeballing me, intent on unspeakably unpleasant things. This was a part of the city that I wouldn't normally have gotten within a mile of. It made most dumps look salubrious.

When I got to the appointed place—a wide area where a large store had been bulldozed to make a flat expanse of land some quarter of a mile square—Rizzie Carter was waiting for me. His face was drawn, his eyes bleary and he looked a mess. Not just his usual mess, but a shook-up mess. Something real bad had squeezed his balls, that was obvious. The big man heaved himself upright, his vast bulk quivering.

"It's a bad one," he said.

"When are they not?" I grunted, studying the place. I could see there had been some recent activity here, the ground churned up by what must have been a whole lot of vehicles. Now there was nothing other than a bunch of cops and medics running around, sifting the soil and occasional bricks for whatever they could unearth.

Rizzie led me across the space to its far end, where several sections of concrete block wall reared up from the obscuring shadows. Graffiti had been daubed on every available space, typically vivid and imaginative, and there were the usual slogans, railing at one religious or political honcho or another. Rizzie waved aside a couple of his men and two guys in white tunics so that we could see what was beyond. I'd seen about as much nastiness in my world as any dozen morticians, but I'll admit what we had here came close to taking the big prize.

Some guy—a youngster of about twenty years—had been pinned up to a wall, spread-eagled and held in place by at least a score of knives. They were unusual weapons, wide-bladed and with ornate handles that gleamed under the police flashlights. Ceremonial? Whoever had done this had first splashed a large pentagram on the wall, the body forming its heart. Blood ran down from the many wounds, congealing in a wide lake on the brick floor below it. Must have been a slow, painful death.

"Yeah, well, it's pretty horrible, Chief," I said. "Nasty way to die. But, hell, you've seen worse. So what's got you shaking in your boots? Not scared of a little black magic, are you?"

He grimaced. "Bloody murder I can handle. The Devil and all his works I can handle. But what's making me nervous as a kitten in a microwave is the fact that sonny boy hanging there is the son of the Mayor of this city."

* * * *

We sat in the Chief's car while the unfortunate victim was unpinned and duly bagged and zipped up for the morgue. This was one case the Chief had to solve, that or his policing days would be over.

"There was a carnival here," he told me, sipping hot coffee. I don't usually share his coffee, which tastes like heated engine oil, but tonight I needed something warm inside me. "Don't know if the kid was visiting it. Seems unlikely. Those knives—pretty sure they belong to one of the acts. Europeans. Which makes them the prime suspects."

"So where's the carnival now?"

"That's just it. No trace. Vanished into thin air. Like it was never here."

One of his men brought us a bag. It contained the set of knives and I examined one of them carefully before letting the forensic experts take them all away.

"Which act was it?" I asked Rizzie.

"Knife throwers," he said, unfurling a small poster. It was the usual gaudy advert for that kind of show. *Count Rudolfo's Hungarian Extravaganza* was emblazoned in thick letters across its top. Rizzie tapped one of the featured names—Dokta Dangerous and the Daggermen. It meant nothing to me.

"I need you to find them, Nick. I need to interview those guys. If they did this, I gotta bring them in and nail *their* asses to the wall. Whatever it takes. You gonna help me with this?"

"A carnival? Jeeze, Chief, you sure do pick 'em."

* * * *

I spent the next day trawling all over for information about the carnival. I found enough references to fill a book, but no one knew where the heck it had gone. I was beginning to get the drift. My guess was, no longer in this world, which figured. You don't pack up a big top, a couple of dozen trailers, rides, animals, you name it, and disappear without someone knowing where you are. Maybe I would have to check out the Pulpworld, the closest world to mine.

Which brought me to Craggy MacFury's Diner, it being Friday. I was hoping to see Montifellini's Magic Bus parked around the corner from the smoking, torpedo-shaped diner, but for once, given it was indeed Friday, there was no sign of it.

"If you're looking for a certain crazy opera singer and that bone-jarring inter-dimensional rust-bucket of his, you're in for a disappointment," MacFury said with a grin.

"So where's Montifellini? Not like him to miss a Friday night special."

"He's all tied up in shenanigans elsewhere. Has been for the last two weeks. Must be important for the likes of him to miss my cooking. You need to see him?"

"Got to get across to the Pulpworld. Fast. Can't call on my usual channels."

I explained some of it to MacFury, but he knew nothing about any carnival. Instead he spent several long minutes ranting about the disgusting qualities of the food stalls associated with such itinerant communities and I nodded quietly, knowing better than to interrupt. Nothing bugged him more than bad food.

Eventually, calming down, he gave a shrug. "There's one possibility you might consider, seeing as how you're in such an all-fired hurry. Montifellini has a nephew. Henry Maclean. Son of Monti's sister, Lucrezia. He's a lively lad. They call him the astral surfer, among other things. Spends more time out of this world than in it, from what I hear."

I suppressed a groan. A surfer? He had to be kidding. And in New York? Must be a lonely guy.

MacFury scribbled down some instructions and went off, grumbling about some people being too damned busy to take the time to stop off for the best food in town. For two pins I would have stayed.

He'd directed me to a bar down along the far eastern end of the harbour, kind of crushed in between some very uncouth places where I knew my face would not be welcome. So I pulled up my collar, drew my hat down and shuffled as inconspicuously as I could down the maze of seedy alleys that led to *Surf City Central*, my unlikely destination. Any port—or bar—in a storm. From outside I could hear the thump of music within, a medley of surfing classics, and for a moment I thought I'd somehow teleported to California.

I went in and felt immediately overdressed, my gear in complete contrast to that of everyone else. My guess was the average age of this packed crowd was nineteen, maybe less. Dudes and babes dressed like it was high summer, long hair flowing, bronzed torsos gleaming—the place looked as if it had been lifted up from the West Coast in midsummer and dropped down here among the sombre harbour side. There were even surfboards—dozens of them—stacked against a wall, like the guys had all ridden in on them.

Naturally I got more than a few surprised looks, but I smiled and waved cheerily, edging my way through the laughing, drinking multitude. The barmen, a trio of them, were as young as the customers, busily dispensing drinks as fast as they could serve them. I have to say, the atmosphere in the place was uncommonly welcoming, if a little left field.

"I'm looking for Henry Maclean," I told one of the barmen. He pointed to where a tall, thin guy with quintessential surfer's blonde hair and sun-kissed skin was animatedly talking to a trio of cute young things. They looked suitably agog at whatever tales of the big surf he was regaling them with, using his hands to demonstrate the curve of the water and the wave tunnels it created.

"I'm Nick Stone—a friend of your uncle," I told him when he paused for breath.

His grin widened. "Hey, man! Montifellini? How's he doing? Haven't seen him in ages." He shook my hand, his grip very firm, his grin even wider. Somehow I had a good feeling about him and I set my usual scepticism about new faces aside.

"Last time I saw him he was fine. Can we talk—privately?"

He looked suddenly very serious, his expression exaggerated but somehow still honest. "Hey, ladies, I have to speak to this dude." They smiled on cue and dissolved into the mass of bodies. Henry was clutching a pint, but it looked like a soft drink, topped with half the contents of an ice bucket and a few chunks of fruit.

"I'll get to the point, Henry. I need to go to the Pulpworld. I'm a private eye and I'm looking for a bunch of people. Normally I'd ask your uncle to help me, but he's busy right now."

"The Pulpworld? Sure, you came to the right guy. *The Deep Green* is always ready to rock and roll. When do you want to leave, man?"

Was this going to be that easy? There had to be a catch. "You're not talking about an airplane?" I said, barely masking my fears.

"Hell, no! *The Deep Green* is the fastest, slickest, slipperiest ship you ever rode in. She's a submarine."

When he took me to his craft, I had to keep reminding myself that I was in a real situation. We left the bar by a side door and went down a tight little alleyway, scattering a few marauding rats on the way to the river. There were a dozen or more big-bellied trawlers in this part of the docks, fat tyres hanging off their sides, decks half buried under piles of ropes and steel mesh pots. Henry led me down a rickety wooden set of steps that dropped us on to a flat, metal surface a few inches above the murky waters of the river. Even in the darkness I could see that the metal had been painted a dark color, which I took to be the deep green of the vessel's name.

Henry bent down and twisted a short spar of metal, using it to lift a circular hatch that allowed him just enough room to climb down on to the steel stairs that dropped vertically from it. "*The Deep Green* welcomes you," he said cheerfully.

I felt like I was sliding down into the gut of a huge fish, but I followed him, pulling the hatch to behind me. I was in a cramped space, brightly lit, surrounded by steel pipes, curling wires and a mess of dials. If this was a submarine, it was not a very big one, I thought. We squeezed our tortuous way along its corridor of dripping pipes that did little to instil confidence. I was okay with ships and boats, up on the surface, but going down under the sea, in something as seemingly leaky as this old tub, was not going to be the happy experience of the day, or indeed, the month.

We reached what he called the control deck, which was basically a wider area with a lowered periscope and a narrow table cluttered up with charts and instruments that looked like they belonged with Admiral Nelson—the one from Trafalgar. Squatting amongst the jumble, wielding a spanner the size of an axe was an ancient, oil-smeared guy, scowling at me like I was some kind of pirate interloper.

"Oil-Gun?" For a minute I thought it was someone I knew, a mechanic, an easy mistake to make in that cluttered space, but when he grinned I could see he was thinner, his face even more creased.

"You know Eddy?" he said.

"Sure," I said. "We've had a few days out together."

"This," interrupted Henry, "is Gottfried Zeitgeist. Former Admiral of the Imperial German War fleet. Just won't admit it, is all."

The old boy—he was seventy if he was a day—struggled to his feet and shook my hand. "Take no notice of young Henry's bullshit. I'm Stan—Sten-Gun Stan. Just another ex-grunt. I fought with Oil-Gun Eddy back in Nam when we were nineteen year old kids. Saved each other's butts several times over. That's where we got our names. I was never anything to do with the freakin' Imperial German whatever."

"I'm Nick Stone. Glad to know you, Stan."

Henry had left us, shouting something about brewing up some coffee. "He's a good kid," Stan told me. "Scatter-brained and erratic as a fart in a thunderstorm, but he's okay. He's convinced himself that I'm not just a good engineer, but I'm really hiding my true identity, like I'm the goddam ex Admiral of the German war machine. I got no more German blood in me than a thoroughbred Apache, but he won't listen. So what brings you aboard? You know this tub can take you anywhere. Places you wouldn't dream of."

Henry arrived with the coffee and we all sipped at it. I gave them a few details about what I was up to and they both nodded sagely, taking it all in, the business as usual.

"Pulpworld?" said Henry. "Straightforward run. I haven't been for a while, but there's places where the surf's good. We can drop Mr Stone off, Admiral, and have some fun at the same time—you must have a few former confederates over there, Admiral. Chew over the good old military days."

"You're nuts," Stan snorted.

Unmoved, Henry asked me, "So you want me to find out about this carnival? Should be easy enough. There's one that sets up regularly. Even if it isn't Count Rudolfo's, they'll know where it is. They're all part of a network, kind of a gypsy fraternity. Okay, let's get our own show on the road. Chocks away, Admiral."

"Fer Chrissakes, Henry, this ain't an aircraft," Stan growled exasperatedly. But Henry was already wriggling past another bank of pipes and steel tubes, and I could hear the unmistakable strains of "Yellow Submarine" drifting back to me as he worked.

"So he's colour-blind?" I said.

Stan shuddered, resignedly getting to work.

I tried to settle back, but as the underwater craft slid away from the harbour and lowered itself into the river, it was difficult not to think of myself being trapped in a leaking, submersible washing machine. I was praying this trip would be a quick one.

An hour limped by and I'd somehow managed to doze off in the thick, cloying heat. I snapped awake when the craft suddenly shook and rolled excessively, as if it had been caught in a particularly turbulent current. I had to grab a hold of pipework on either side of me to save myself being swung feet upwards like an astronaut in a weightless space pod. By the time I rectified myself, Henry was grinning at me.

"It's okay, Mr Stone. It's a Swallower."

Now there was a name guaranteed to pump up the adrenalin level. "A *Swallower*? And just what in hell would that be, Henry?"

He scratched his tousled blonde mop. "Don't know for sure. Never actually seen one. It's either some kind of oceanic black hole, like they have out in deep space, or more likely a mother of a whale-thing. Whatever, it'll gulp us down, spin us about some and then evacuate us out the other end—"

I gaped at him. "You are kidding me."

"Sometimes we have to use a tin fish to ease our passage. You know, blow our way out, but that's okay."

Something rattled to the front of my memory. "A tin fish? You're talking torpedo here?"

"Sure. The Admiral keeps a few primed and ready to go at all times. Whatever, once we stop churning about in this thing's gut, we'll be through and into the Pulpworld. Sound like a plan?"

"Remind me to get the bus on the return journey," I muttered, but Henry was busy again and a moment later I saw him undress and slip into a skin-tight wet suit that looked like it had been painted on.

The Deep Green performed several more undersea somersaults, somehow avoided rupturing its maze of pipes, and then seemed to stabilize. More dazed and confused than Robert Plant ever was, I vaguely heard Stan shouting out something about having 'ripped through'—presumably to our destination.

"You need some air, Mr Stone," said Henry, taking me to the vertical ladder that led up to the surface hatch. He scrambled up it, complete with—get this—a *surfboard.* It was jet black and had the open maw of a shark painted into its nose end. I followed its tail upwards and into a flattish seascape, washed by brilliant moonlight, and stood on the gently oscillating deck of the submarine. The air was very cool, but as welcome as an ice cold glass of beer.

I could see a chain of lights on the near horizon. Henry pointed. "The Admiral never lets me down. We've crossed. Why don't you get yourself a deck chair from below and make yourself comfortable, Mr Stone. I'll go and do some reconnaissance. Be back before you know it." He said it as if inviting me to sit and sunbathe on a beach. And he was not joking. Right—at five a.m.?

I just nodded. He was studying a rolling bank of sea mist, grey against the backdrop of night and as it drifted across the water, swirling and twisting like spilled silk, he lowered his board, waiting. I was about to point out that there was no tide, ergo no surf—the sea was as flat as a proverbial pancake—when he gave a whoop and pushed the board off the submarine, jumping on to it and balancing lightly. To my amazement, the board rose with the eddy of mist and in no time, Henry was riding not a wave of water, but a curling bank of mist.

"Crazy how he does that," said Stan beside me. "They call him the astral surfer. No one can ride a wind wave like that guy." We both gawped at the surfer as he rose higher on the eddying mist, which could have been solid given Henry's amazing exhibition. He glided down at speed into an aerial tunnel, blurring and then disappearing.

Stan slapped me on the back. "We can leave him to it. Time for an early breakfast." He took me back down below, where I was surprised to learn that I had built up a hearty appetite.

* * * *

"There's a carnival there and it's Rudolfo's, all right," said Henry, back with us a couple of hours later. He downed a plate of bacon and eggs like it was the condemned man's last meal and washed it down with almost an entire pot of coffee. "I spoke to some of the roustabouts. And those guys you want to interview, Dokta Dangerous and the Daggermen—they're holed up in a coupla caravans. Look like the genuine articles to me, Mr Stone. Good old Hungarian boys. When d'ya want to go in?"

Stan was grinning at my expression—I'd been looking uneasily at the shark-nosed surfboard beside us. "It's okay, Mr Stone, I can take the sub in to the docks, just like in your own New York."

"Sure," said Henry. "Plenty of time for surfing later, huh?"

"Of course," I said. Didn't seem any point in arguing.

Not long afterwards, with dawn smearing the eastern skies in a confusion of red and orange light, we stepped ashore in the Pulpworld's equivalent of New York. I'd been here before, many times, and you never knew what was around the corner. I agreed to meet up with Henry later in the day and left him to his own devices on *The Deep Green.*

I'd been trying to figure what my approach was going to be. Dokta Dangerous and his troupe were, possibly, a bunch of killers and if so, they'd make short work of someone like me snooping around them. On the other hand, they might have been framed. I decided to go for the direct approach. If these guys took a dislike to me, they'd at least have to be subtle about kicking me out. So I found my way to the carnival, which was camped in a derelict area, its rides,tents and caravans clustered there like a small township.

At first when I asked for Dokta D, no one wanted to play ball. So I started grumbling about working for the FBI and maybe having to bring a whole squad in here. It got results and I was sent to a caravan that was painted every colour known to man, with amazingly ornate wheels and patterns that confused the eye. Staring at it for too long could send a guy nuts. Its low door creaked open and I climbed the steps and went inside.

It was surprisingly roomy, its walls hung with thick rugs and carpets, very expensive looking. In back of the caravan I could see several tall shapes, dark-haired men, bare-armed and tattooed, faces calm but their stares fixed on me in less than neighbourly fashion. Sitting on the central table was what I first took to be a kid, his legs drawn up under him, arms clutching his knees. When he spoke, I realised he was a man, a dwarf, maybe four feet tall.

"Nick Nightmare," he said, his Hungarian accent rich and deep. "I heard about you." I wasn't about to ask him where from.

"I take it you're Dokta Dangerous," I said with a nod. "Don't like to butt in, but I need a little chat."

He grinned, revealing a set of amazingly white teeth, and ran a gnarled hand through his thick, black locks. "Of course. What can I do for you?"

"Your carnival was in my world recently. You left kinda quickly. Want to tell me about it?"

"Who's employing you?"

"The Good Guys. They had some trouble back there. Something very messy." I pulled out a small cloth bundle from inside my coast and unwrapped it. One of the knives that had been used to pin up the Mayor's son twinkled in the oil lamplight.

"We know about that," said the dwarf, his expression changing, his eyes cold. "It's a very good fake. I can show you. Listen, can you hear that blow-fly behind you? Well, that knife can't do this." His right hand moved in a blur and something flashed vividly. There was a thump behind me. I turned slowly and saw that the knife the little fellar had thrown was embedded in one of the wooden panels of the wall. And it had very neatly split a blow-fly clean in two.

I whistled in admiration. "That's what I call accuracy."

The Dokta favoured me with another grin. "Only a true knife of the Daggermen could do that. Try it. You'll find that knife you brought perfectly serviceable, Mr Nightmare, but to us, it's a toy. And as I said, a fake. It and the others that were used on the Mayor's son were all fakes. The killing was made to look like the work of my people and me."

I nodded. "You could have stayed and talked it over with the cops."

"No. The hoax was very elaborate and I suspect it would have worked. At best we would have suffered the indignity of a protracted questioning. We have better things to do with our time."

"Sure. So—who did the killing?"

His face again hardened. "Are you sure you want to know?"

"They sent me to find out. Maybe even bring back the killer, if he's here."

He laughed a short bark and for once the men behind him came to life, also laughing, but it didn't warm me up. I felt like I was putting my arm into a snake pit.

"What we are talking about isn't human," said the dwarf. "It has many names. You would call it a demon, I suppose. An agent of Satan. In fact, there are several of them. We know them as the Angels of Malice. Terrible creatures, wielding very dangerous powers. Not the kind of beings that you can—arrest—and march back to your world."

"So why did they frame you for the killing?"

"They want to recruit me and my Daggermen. The Angels of Malice are always hunting, always searching out those who they think can strengthen their black crusade. We spurned their offers. We have our own gods. Incensed, the Angels of Malice tried to use coercion. They have threatened us with worse things if we continue to rebuff them. I promise you, Mr Nightmare, we shall do."

"Glad to hear it. But it poses a problem for me. I have to report back to the police in my world. If I tell them that some kind of demon is responsible, they won't buy it. Not without proof. So how do I provide them with it? Remember, we're talking about the Mayor's son here. *He's* gonna want to know the truth."

The dwarf swung his short legs off the table and dangled them like pendulums as if it aided his thinking. "There's only one way to teach them the truth. The truth is more powerful than a thousand lies. An old Hungarian saying."

"I'm all ears."

"You may wish you were deaf when I tell you what you must do. You must achieve the near impossible. You must overcome one of the Angels of Malice and take it back. Show your Mayor and the police. If you can do this, the other Angels of Malice will shun your world. A triumph, Mr Nightmare. Are you prepared to attempt such a bold venture?"

I tried a little bravado. "So where do I find these Angels of Malice?"

"You cannot face them alone. That is, you can, but they would likely incinerate you in the blink of an eye. Doubtless you have protection. It won't be enough, not here. We can help you. After all, we would be glad to see the Angels of Malice thwarted and if you were successful, they would focus their attention elsewhere."

"I'll settle for that."

"The leader of the Angels of Malice has asked for a meeting with us, a final discussion in the wake of the murder—a last chance for us to capitulate before he does his worst. It is unlikely he will be expecting a trap. To some extent, he will be unguarded. He is a very arrogant creature. If we fail, however, it will be the end of the Daggermen, and of you, Mr Nightmare. At least, in the worlds we know."

* * * *

The appointed place was at the end of an abandoned jetty that ran out into a run-down part of the harbour, long since disused, the black waters choked with rusted, half-submerged hulks. At the end of the jetty there was a circular area, a former landing zone some fifty yards across, at one end a crumpled crane, leaning over at a crazy angle, smeared in seagull crap that gleamed in the glow of the nearby harbour lights. It was very exposed, which is why the Angel of Malice had chosen it—doubtless he wanted to be sure he had a three sixty degree view of everything around him. A cold wind blew in from the Atlantic and I could see the white of breaking waves out in the slate grey of the bay.

The Daggermen positioned themselves strategically around the perimeter of the derelict circular loading point, seven of them including the Dokta. I knew that they all carried long knives that were more like swords. It didn't take a genius to figure out they were weapons of power.

These Hungarians had been mixed up in demonology and all the other kinds of sorcery for millennia and they drew on magic that was outside the knowledge of most people.

It was why the Angel of Malice wanted to recruit them. I'd asked the Dokta about it when he was supervising the preparations for the meeting. "If he could control us and use our powers," the Dokta had told me, "he would control the carnival. It would enable him to extend his influence more easily. The Angels of Malice are always seeking ways to burrow into human affairs, like cancer invading a body. Subtle but deadly. We have fought them for centuries."

I'd been given various items—a thin, silver chain, a two inch statuette of some kind of forest creature, a sort of faun, ugly as sin and a necklace. Now, normally you'd have to get a bunch of toughs to hold me down before you got me to wear a necklace, but here, in these circumstances, I wasn't going to argue. I'd suggested to the Dokta that I called on some of my contacts—in Pulpworld, I have many reliable friends—but he'd demurred.

"We use the old magic," he said. He was arranging for a large vat of something very oily and foul-smelling to be boiled up outside his caravan. When the bubbling contents had cooled down a mite, his men dipped their arms into the mess, up to their elbows. I had to do the same and it was only when I'd got the disgusting gunk right up to my own elbows that I recognised the smell. This revolting concoction was comprised mainly of *blood.*

"Don't be concerned," said the dwarf, with an evil grin. "It's not human."

So that was okay. Not human. I didn't ask. I just rolled the sleeves of my shirt down and put my coat back on. Even so, it didn't hide the stench.

Now, taking up my position in the shadows behind the Dokta, I could still smell the muck on my arms. The harbour stank of oil, weed and other sea-type stenches, but the blood I carried won out. We waited. The moon, three quarters full, broke occasionally from the clouds, adding to the spectral nature of the area. The Daggermen were like statues, their long knives still out of sight. I was beginning to doze, when I saw movement.

Up on the crane. A shadow detached itself from its top, slipping down through the tangled spars, soundless, agile as a spider. That was an image I didn't want to think about. I like spiders as much as small flying insects do. We waited as the creature lowered itself to the ground. It was taller than most men, its body wreathed in darkness that completely obscured whatever it was wearing. Only its head was visible, a gaunt skull, devoid of hair, almost white. A dozen horror movies sprang to mind, but this wasn't amusing. The Angel of Malice exuded an atmosphere that was deeply disturbing, like heat from an oven, different to any kind of power I'd ever come across before.

As it walked calmly across the circular area, its feet made no sound, as if it was gliding—that and the fact that the whole area was covered in a number of tarpaulins that the Daggermen had spread there earlier in the day. They were black and blotched here and there with oil stains and as far as anyone knew, they'd been lying around for a long time. The Angel of Malice paid them no heed. He just went to the centre of the area and stood very still, his gaze fixed on the pint-sized Hungarian.

"Ferenc Halmosi, my old friend!" said the Angel of Malice. Its teeth were a brilliant white—they'd have sold a million tubes of toothpaste. "You came. Perhaps you've reconsidered my offer, after all." The voice was harsh, but somehow very seductive, part of the creature's power, I guessed. "Sensible of you to prevent any more unpleasantness between us. I trust you are ready to capitulate?"

"I will never surrender to you, Urruzaal, you should know that. My ancestors have fought your kind since time began. It shall be so with my descendants."

The Angel's face changed, the epitome of hatred, agony, all that stuff. It wasn't good to look at. "Ah, so it has to be a contest of wills. Very well. I expected as much."

The dwarf raised his arm slightly and around the circle I saw his men take out their weapons and hold them before them like firebrands. He did the same and the Angel of Malice regarded all seven blades, its eyes ablaze, but whether with anger or delight, I couldn't tell. As it watched, the men pulled back their sleeves and even in this faint light, the dried blood was evident. The Angel of Malice lifted its head and sniffed the night air like a huge hound. It had caught the scent of the blood and now it was definitely pissed off.

"Demon blood!" For a moment it looked nonplussed, but then it laughed, a truly horrible sound. Everything about this monster suggested pain, so it was well named. "You're a fool, Ferenc, if you think you can bind me. You need more than the blood."

The Dokta bent his small frame and hauled aside the tarpaulin he was standing on, to reveal a section of what he and his men had laboriously painted across the whole of the stone floor of the area earlier—in demon blood, naturally. It was an elaborate pentacle.

The Angel of Malice hissed like a steam engine, glaring at the tarpaulin where it was standing. My guess was it could see beneath it now, and understood the extent of the painted workings. I knew that the Dokta had written a name in its very centre, though it had meant nothing to me at the time he daubed it there. I knew it now—Urruzaal.

At another signal from the dwarf, he and his men stepped forward, three strides, their long knives pointed directly at the dark figure. Urruzaal emitted an animal howl of fury and pulled from its robes a weapon of its own. It was some kind of short staff, its head the size of a tennis ball. Weird light coruscated from it. Somewhere between the seven knives and Urruzaal's staff, light fizzed and popped like some kind of miniature electrical storm. It was spreading, the light intensifying: I could make out shapes writhing within it, hurtling around, claws spread, mouths gaping. Urruzaal was ringed by the incandescence, turning this way and that in an attempt to drive the light back at the wielders of the blades.

The Dokta had told me that this would happen and had primed me for my part in this colossal battle of wills. I bent down and reached under another flap of tarpaulin, pulling out a metal lance, a couple of metres long, another item in the Dokta's supernatural arsenal. It was deceptively lightweight but beautifully balanced. The Angel of Malice was too preoccupied trying to blast aside the weapons of the seven Daggermen to notice me. I waited for the roaring within the circle of light to reach thunderous levels and at a cry from the dwarf, stepped forward.

Urruzaal saw the movement and turned his frightful gaze—no longer remotely human—on me. A vampire would have been a whole lot more attractive. I concentrated on the lance and my target area. A couple of steps and I threw the weapon: I made like an Olympian and put every ounce of my strength into that cast, adding to its weight my fear. The shaft actually *sang* as it shot across the space between us, tearing through the whirling lights, striking its target—Urruzaal's chest—plumb in the centre. I'd put such a heck of an effort into the throw that the lance tore through the body of the Angel of Malice like a knife through butter and came bursting out of the creature's back. I'd done a good job.

Or so I thought. Actually, I'd messed up. I was supposed to spit Urruzaal's body like a piece of meat on a sheesh kebab, thus rendering him temporarily useless, at which time the Daggermen would swarm over him like leeches in a bowl of blood. Instead my throw had been so hard that the goddam lance went right on through, out the other side and clattered impotently on the tarpaulin several feet away. I did get the consolation prize, though—Urruzaal screamed in pain and staggered to one knee.

The Dokta and his six men charged inward, but their assault was met with powerful resistance. Even down on one knee, the Angel of Malice was amazingly powerful. It held up its staff, which absorbed all the cuts, swipes and blows that the Daggermen could unleash. The crazy stalemate threatened to go on for the rest of the night. I would have made a try for the fallen lance, but Urruzaal was wise to that and I couldn't get round him: something coiled out of the air close to his feet and smothered the weapon in a wreath of shadows. Neither I nor the Daggermen were going to be able to penetrate that cloud.

Urruzaal was gradually showing signs of regaining his former strength and slowly he rose up to his full height. My guess was he was going to make one final push and blast all of us to Hell and damnation, and there didn't seem like there was much we could do to stop him. Around the far edges of the circular stone area, a thick mist was gathering, kinda like there was something out there that was *enjoying* this mayhem on the dock. The mist curled upwards and shaped itself into a wave more than a billow of cloud.

The Dokta abruptly lurched backwards. I could see that the balance of power had shifted. Urruzaal was definitely getting the upper hand. We'd missed our chance. I saw the creature's face contort with unholy glee, then change as a shape came gliding in over the dock, riding on that rolling bank of mist like a manta ray. It took me a minute to figure out what it was.

Henry Maclean had surfed in, his shark-faced board skimming the air just above the stone. With one swift twist, Henry aimed the board directly at the legs of the Angel of Malice. The board sliced into the creature, homing in like a missile and Urruzaal was knocked sideways, shrieking out curses that were thick with its own pain. The Dokta and his men and I watched the fallen monster struggling to get up again, like a crab with a broken shell. Urruzaal raised his head and howled out his fury, curses flaming like fire.

Henry Maclean was having the surf of his life. He gave his own version of a rebel yell and curved back into the centre of the area, this time propelling his board at Urruzaal's exposed neck. The shark nose cracked against muscle and bone and Urruzaal's head flopped over sideways, the spinal column broken clean in two by the majestic pass of the astral surfer. The Angel of Pain toppled to the ground like a beached fish. Its fingers went into brief spasm, there were a series of particularly revolting curses, then all was still.

I noticed that the lance I had hurled earlier was now free of its protective cloud, so I went over to it, lifted it and wasted no more time in ramming it into Urruzaal's fallen form. I felt the point of the lance bite into the stone floor of the dock. This time the creature was pinned like a butterfly to a card. The dwarf and his men were at my side, unable to resist giving a unified cheer.

"Is this thing dead?" I asked them as Henry came zipping in, dismounting and picking up his board in one dramatic flourish.

The Dokta shook his head. "The body was once a human, chosen to host the Angel of Malice. Urruzaal remains alive, inside the body, but it is trapped. We will complete the work and seal it in, so that it cannot infest a new host. The creature cannot be killed, but it can be contained and rendered powerless."

"Henry," I said, much relieved, "your timing is perfection itself."

The young man beamed, tossing back those extravagant blonde locks, like some mad Celtic god. But right now, mad Celtic gods were fine by me. "Get a load of that lance! That's what I'm talking about. You think these guys would do a trade? The Admiral has some neat stuff—"

"I don't think so, Henry. You probably don't want to mess with it anyway. And you've got that surfboard—what the hell else do you need?"

He laughed. "You bet. That was some mist! Don't usually get currents like that other than in the sea. What a rush! You want to try this, Mr Stone? It'll blow you away."

"Probably not right now, Henry. I need to get this case cleared up. I have to get this fallen angel back to my Chief of Police. Any ideas how we do that?"

Henry laughed. "Sure. The Admiral will accommodate us." He pointed to the edge of the dock and I wasn't surprised to see a bloated metal shape bobbing up from the murky waters—a deep green metal shape. Its deck hatch clanged open and Sten-Gun Stan emerged, jumping on to the dock and coming over to us a little apprehensively.

I turned to the Dokta and his men. They had already started exposing parts of the corpse and they used their knives to carve what I took to be runes of power in the white flesh, strange numeric designs like digital, binding chains. After they put their knives away, the dwarf smiled at me, his teeth gleaming. "I wish you luck in your own world, Mr Stone. Be warned, however—Urruzaal will never rest. You must seal him away carefully. Keep him far from fire, it is his life blood. A deep lake, perhaps, submerged in cold water, or in the heart of a glacier. That would hold him for an eternity."

A glacier. In New York? Yeah, that would be a challenge. I glanced at Sten-Gun Stan.

"I'll put him in one of the torpedo tubes," he said casually, like he was about to load a few sacks of grain. "Once you've done with him, we'll go out to Arctic waters and fire him into a deep water crevasse."

* * * *

We got back to my New York uneventfully and it wasn't long after I reported to Rizzie Carter that I found myself down at the local morgue. Dokta Dangerous, sans Daggermen, had joined me and I was given the dubious honour of doing the (fast) talking. Urruzaal had been bundled—complete with transfixing lance—into a makeshift coffin, which now resided on a bare metal table. The cold room was garishly lit and the group of people who stood round the coffin could have passed for a bunch of extras from a stalk and slash movie.

Central to the montage was the Mayor, Johnny Wizacki, a lean, mean-looking guy of forty who liked very expensive clothes. He had taken a brief look at the now shrivelled body in the coffin, scowled with justifiable disgust and waited irritably for someone to tell him what the holy hell was going on. Rizzie Carter took a back seat, hands in his pockets, mouth closed, and studied the scrubbed floor tiles like a man waiting to be sentenced by a judge wearing a black cap.

"This was no ordinary murder," I began. "Your son, Mr Wizacki, got himself inadvertently mixed up in a turf war and was the unwitting victim of a particularly vicious gang."

The Mayor's icy glare never wavered. I moved on. "The focus of the latest conflict was a carnival called *Count Rudolfo's Hungarian Extravaganza* and its right to run here in the city. Some of the local Mob, and I don't know the details, or the names, hired the guy in the coffin to do their bullying. They wanted *Rudolfo's* out of the city, that or pay up fifty per cent of the takings. Rudolfo wouldn't play ball, so the Mob applied some pressure. They had their assassin rig up a high profile killing to make it look like Rudolfo's people were responsible. That's where Mr Halmosi here, comes in. He, as Dokta Dangerous, together with his Daggermen troupe, are the world's outstanding knife-throwing act."

The Mayor winced and I moved on again, a little more speedily. "The Mob's assassin had a set of knives made—very realistic copies of Mr Halmosi's knives—so good that only Mr Halmosi and his team would have known they were fakes. Your son was murdered with these, so that it looked for certain like Mr Halmosi was responsible for a death that would bring the whole of the city down on his neck. Chief Carter smelled a rat, though, shrewd operator that he is. He needed someone on the inside, which is why he asked me to do some snooping on his behalf. I talked to Mr Halmosi and that's when I figured what had really happened. No one was going to believe Mr Halmosi unless we caught the real killer.

"Well, sir, we did that, but it was like cornering a rat in a drain. The assassin put up one hell of a fight and you can see the result for yourself.

He didn't live to tell the tale." I pointed to the coffin. "And he didn't squeal on the big shots who employed him. It's a dead end."

The Mayor walked quietly over to me and stood with his face very close to mine. "Nice try, Mr Stone, but I smell bullshit."

I was about to launch into a garbled defence of my revelations, but ironically the Mayor dug me out of a hole without realising it. "My son was a goddam moron—a gambling, whore-mongering, dope-sniffing moron! I told him time and time again, keep your friggin' nose out of the crap! You got a good future, don't screw it up by mixing with the hoodlums of this town. Did he listen? Nah. Couldn't tell the jerk nothin'. His mother disowned him, you hear me? All those years of that love and fuss—wasted. What can I say? The kid didn't deserve to be carved up like he was, but it would never have happened if he'd listened to his old man. So you don't need to cover up for him."

"I'm sorry, Mr Wizacki," I murmured.

He clapped me on the shoulder. "You did a good job. You, too, Chief. This town needs men like you. Listen, guys, I don't want this business blown up in a courtroom. Not good for the family name. Hell, I'm no saint, but I've got plans—nice plans—for the city. It wouldn't be a good time for my family to be dragged through the mud. I'm sure you can dispose of that sack of turds, eh? I'll lay on a decent funeral for my kid. I'll think up something for his death. You guys just forget the whole affair."

The Chief nodded understandingly. The Mayor turned to the tiny figure beside me and shook him by the hand. "Listen, Mr Halmosi, tell your boss that his carnival can have the run of New York for as long as he wants. You get any kind of trouble, you talk to me. Understand?"

The Dokta grinned his best Hungarian grin and it followed the Mayor all the way out of the door. "We owe you many thanks," he said to me. "We have rid ourselves of a terrible enemy, and we would like to repay you, Mr Stone. How can we do this?"

I went to the coffin. "The lance," I said. "Is it safe to remove it?"

The Dokta nodded. "Urruzaal is trapped in the body, held there by the sigils and spells that we have painted over the flesh of his host. You desire the lance?"

"You never know when these things will come in useful." ▲

NecRomance

by Frederick J. Mayer

Dedicated to Clark Ashton Smith

"A Lost Chapter From The Book Of Eibon"

Barbarian horde of near hairless
paleful skin
over running even mountain cold
wasted lands
their scything sharp abyss kissing swords
found within
even Sfatlicllp's own consorts from
Voormis clans.
Hyperborean lords near fearless
baleful in
this on-going slaughter oh so bold
by these bands
their birth unknown but that towards
evening sin...
Ebonian crystal sorceress
KuMiHo
owner says "dead will of you cuckold"
necromance
spells and philtres of desire dark lore
ever so
said of hearts eaten protection from
such sex dance.
Beastian plants sup cannibal flesh
of Tcho
consummate grimore knowledge old
and by chance
gain anthropophagic made force for
attack blow
Homofloran man forms early this

night now are
more human than mandrake design told
go to East
from setting sun take devour that shore
mind guide Zhar
be yours given cosmic "steel" to come
kill & feast.
Guardian of garden of Eden bliss
under Star
Infernal as flower evil sowed
is as least
fire fruit flora meretrix faithful swore
lovers are...
Euglenans close house of black gneiss
mage therein
Eibon in rapture female cajoled
darkly sans
live concubine carcass leans forwards
ghoulish grin
forbidden fruit tells scourge source comes from
offers plans.
Mhu Thulan magician knows coitus
scheme given
dire incantations romancing mold
lewd commands
ebullient sorcery shield wards
now begin
Stygian expulsion Eucharist
eat to go
teraphim necrophilic hold
cracked monstrance
deviant genomic predator
free from so
exorcist Quachil Uttaus come
age vengeance.
Black barbaric blossoms' detritus
roots of foe
decomposing bile weapons corrode
bane silence
deflowering expelling no more
dust below.

The Music of Bleak Entrainment

by Gary A. Braunbeck

You should see the expression on your face right now—all the trouble you've been through in order to get the clearance to interview me, and I start off by talking about household appliances and math instead of those twelve people I killed. Not that anyone gives more of damn about them now than they did ten years ago—after all, what'd the world lose? A dozen mental patients who were a drain on society's pocketbook. None of them were ever going to be released, they were lifers, and as far as I ever knew none of them had any living family.

Huh? Do I feel *bad* about it? What the fuck kind of Journalism 101 question is that? No, I don't feel bad—I feel *horrible* about it. You weren't there, you didn't see those faces, those eyes…Christ. Those lonely, isolated, frightened eyes.

You want to know something that the news reports back then never mentioned? *Not a one of them tried to run away*, to get to safety. It was like shooting tin ducks at a carnival booth. Hell, some of them seemed to *welcome* it.

I tried to explain everything to the authorities at the time but I was pretty…out of control. No, wait, scratch that—I was so fucking *scared* it was like I wasn't even *me* any longer, I was trapped somewhere inside myself just watching it all happen and…ah, never mind. But I'll tell you the same thing I told my lawyer and the court—I was *not* insane. Not for one second.

As you can tell from our posh surroundings and this lovely canvas jacket with the wraparound arms that I'm sporting, they didn't believe me.

Look, it all started because Steve and I got this idea about using entrainment to visually illustrate how the human body can—

—excuse me? Oh, sorry.

It's been proven that externally-imposed sound vibrations can have a profound influence on our physiology. We've all experienced this phenomenon—it's called entrainment. Say you're sitting in your kitchen trying to balance your checkbook and you begin to notice that your shoulders are hunched up and your back is tighter than normal. Suddenly the refrigerator snaps off and you heave a sigh of relief. Your shoulders drop, your back loosens up, and your whole breathing pattern changes. What do you think just happened? Certain biological rhythms have unconsciously "entrained" themselves to the 60 cycle hum of the refrigerator's motor.

Right—*sound* caused your body to temporarily alter itself from within.

Think you can bear with me for a minute or two while I bore you with some specifics?

No, *Steve* was the Music major. I was the Physics dude.

I was doing some research into the work of Hans Jenny. He was a Swiss doctor, artist, and researcher who helped pioneer the field of Cymatics—which is basically a very specified and intensely focused form of entrainment, geared toward using sound and vibrational waves to heal the human body. He followed the work of a German physicist and acoustician named Ernst Chladni who, toward the end of the 18th Century, created intricate sand patterns by vibrating a steel plate with a violin bow. Jenny employed the modern technology of the day to carry out more precisely replicable experiments. He used a sine wave generator and a speaker to vibrate various powders, pastes, and liquids, and succeeded in making visible the subtle power through which sound *physically structures* matter.

Now, imagine hearing a tone, and watching as sound waves involute an inert blob of kaolin paste, animating it through various phases in a nearly perfect replica of cellular division—or watching as a pile of sand is transformed into life-like flowing patterns, mirroring fractals—the symmetrical geometric forms found in nature—simply by *audible vibration*.

Jenny described our bodies as being "nested hierarchies of vibrational frequencies" which appear as discreet systems functioning within larger, more complicated systems, which themselves are contained within even larger and more complex vibrational structures, right? *All physical existence* is determined by vibrational frequencies and their formative effects on matter.

You can view the whole universe in this way, from sub-atomic particles to the most intricate life forms, to the nebulae and galaxies themselves—all are resonating fields of pulsating energy in constant interaction with one another. The science of it all aside, I find it profoundly moving to think that sound in all its forms might very well be the glue that holds our consensual reality together.

I was really excited about this when I was explaining it to Steve, and I didn't want to bore him, so I started putting it in musical terms. The universe exists—beneath all or most other layers of perception—as essentially a vibrating-string note among a wild symphony of equally vibrating harmonic or non-harmonic quantum notes being played on similar strings—

—*yes*, like an orchestra. Exactly like an orchestra.

Steve asked me if it were possible to show him how this process worked, so he and I repeated one of Jenny's early experiments. We placed a small wooden ring containing about 20 cc. of kaolin paste on top of a magnifying lens, then attached a crystal to the lens and applied a small sound current, creating a specific vibration…which can vary, depending upon the frequency or the current if you apply electricity directly. Just as a speaker vibrates, displacing air and creating specific sound waves according to the frequencies it's subjected to, the vibrating crystal transmitted its oscillations from the sound current frequencies, through the lens, and directly into the paste sample. Light was projected up from beneath the lens, through the paste, and into a camera lens looking down from above. I was able to photograph the disturbances—the standing wave patterns—created in the paste as it vibrated in response to the sine waves—the music—to which it was subjected. Steve played some of his recent composition on the cello, which was attached to the lens by a string of piano wire. A bit on the primitive side, I admit, but effective nonetheless. The moment was captured, then it was just a simple matter of instantly freezing the shape the paste assumed and encasing it in amber.

No, we *didn't* freeze sound, we froze a specific instance of sound physically altering matter.

The next thing we did was even simpler. We ran the music through a basic computer visualizing program—you know, one of those extras that come bundled in with music playing software? Right. We decided to use the Fractal Pattern option, and I gotta tell you, the flow of images that accompanied the music was quite lovely. So now we had both the music and the fractal visualization for sensory input.

This really got us both going.

Steve had just finished a new composition—he hadn't given it a title yet, he always sucked at titles, anyway—but he was stressing over it because something was missing. He kept lamenting how it was impossible to gauge a person's emotional reaction to music, aside from what they themselves would tell you after hearing it.

I thought of Jenny and Chladni.

I thought of all the Cymatic equipment gathering dust in the Bioacoustics Department.

And I thought about how both Steve and I were in danger of losing our scholarships if we didn't come up with a term-end project that would floor everyone.

Have you heard the piece of music that Steve composed for the initial phase of the experiment? No? Too bad—it's a beautiful piece of work.

It begins with an acoustic guitar rhythmically picking out four simple notes, the sound of raindrops pinging against a cold autumn window, four austere notes that remain constant and never change, then builds in musical and emotional intensity, culminating in a three-minute finale where the guitar is joined and then *replaced* by an orchestra whose individual instruments compliment the underlying four-note foundation in the same way that wind, thunder, and lightning accompany a sudden spring downpour. The music is both glorious and sad, tinged at the edges with a certain disquieting darkness, an unnamable fear that we all experience during strong storms; as this section nears its end the four-note foundation suddenly stops, leaving only the melancholy musings of the other instruments, which mix into one another like the stray thoughts of one for whom the rhythm of the rain brings a sense of peace, but when robbed of that rhythm, when finding there is no longer the hypnotic pinging of those raindrops against the cold autumn window, is left to their own devices, slowly succumbing to the sadness and disquieting fear that that the sound of the rain had helped them avoid facing. In these final moments one could close one's eyes and easily picture the drab grey sky and the cheerless, soaked, bleak world.

Initially, we decided to use individuals, people we knew. They'd come into one of the acoustically-tiled rehearsal rooms and sit in a chair, I'd hook them up to the EKG and EEG machines, and then Steve would play a recording of the piece for them while the fractal program was projected through an LCD screen. The EKG and EEG machines would measure their physiological reactions during the music while watching the LCD, and that was the extent of their participation.

After three or four people had done this, both Steve and I realized that, well, most of our friends had high blood pressure, for one thing, but more than that, there was no way to holistically quantify the results—at least, not the way we were doing it. All we had was a series of readouts to show how these people's bodies reacted to the music, nothing to prove that Cymatic theory was even applicable.

Then Steve got this bright idea about incorporating synthesizers into the experiment. I had to do a lot of begging and fast talking to the Bioacoustics Department heads, and I have *no* idea what Steve said to the bigwigs of the Music Department, but we were both given access to the equipment we needed.

I got the use of an EEG—and EKG-measurement/interpreter that served as a conduit between the EEG and EKG machines and the synthesizer bank. The M/I had once been used for Cymatic experimentation—specifically the direct estimations of the main parameters of neurons—time constant of integration, level of internal noise, etc.—received by the cells, or for our purposes, the auditory reactions located on different levels—or in this case, the subjects—hooked up to the system.

I'm sorry, I'm getting off on a technical tangent. I'll try to put it in simpler terms, but I make no promises. After all, I'm crazy, aren't I?

The basic experiment remained unchanged. A subject would come into one of the rooms and we'd hook them up to the EEG and EKG machines and then have them listen to the music and watch the fractal program, only instead of just getting a simple readout of their physiological reactions during the music, those reactions were filtered through the M/I into the synthesizer's computer where they were interpreted as an actual auditory event.

The computer then took all of this catalogued information and fed it into the output ports of the synthesizer banks, which—employing the information received from the M/I—assigned each set of recorded physiological reactions a specific musical scale, as well as a virtual instrument to play the individual notes within that scale.

This took all of maybe forty minutes—the piece was short, otherwise we'd've been looking at days, even weeks, of data processing. Anyway, the person was asked to come back in an hour, and when they did, they got to listen to a musical interpretation of their physiological reaction to the original piece of music, as well as watch a visual representation *of* those physiological reactions.

Steve and I were both stunned that it worked.

So we took it a step further. After we'd done this with half a dozen test subjects, we decided, just for shits and giggles, to play all six reaction pieces simultaneously. Now, all of them were in the same key—the computer had been programmed to make certain of that—but that's where any similarities in the pieces should have ended. But that wasn't the case.

Incredible as it sounds, when all six of those reaction recordings were played back simultaneously, they *fit together*. It was as if someone had taken a pre-existing piece of music and broken it up into six isolated parts. Individually, these six reaction recordings were pleasant enough, okay? No real melody to speak of, but not discordant, either. Each one was like a musical tone poem.

But when we combined them, they created an almost *complete* piece of music.

Are you getting this, Miss Reporter? Think about everything I've told you up to this point and apply it to those results.

All consciousness is connected as a primary wavefront phenomenon that allows us not only to resonate to such notes, but to play a few of our own back here where we sit among the other quantum woodwinds!

Which means, like it or not, that there exists some *base* wavefront to which all others are connected. I wouldn't go so far as to call it God, but…it gave me pause, that's for certain.

But it didn't stop there. We noticed there were sounds on the periphery of the music, soft chattering noises, so Steve made a master recording and started to isolate the sounds. It never occurred to us to play it with the visualization program—we were too excited about the music and the sounds. Maybe if it *had* occurred to us to run it with the fractal program, thing would've…never mind. Shoulda-woulda-coulda. You could make yourself crazy cataloguing all the what-ifs.

So we started concentrating on the Cymatic side of the experiment. If these wavefronts, these vibrational frequencies, could also be employed to heal the body, then why not go for it? We'd proven—at least to ourselves—that there was a definite *structure* underneath all of this, so the question became, how do we *apply* it?

We didn't have to wait too long for our answer. Of the six people who participated in the original phase of the experiment, *four* of them reported that they'd been feeling better since doing so. One girl who suffered from migraine headaches—she told us she got at least one every two weeks, on average—told us that she hadn't gotten a headache in almost a month. Another guy, a halfback on the university football team, had been having severe problems with his back and was on the verge of being cut. *He* came back to tell us that whatever was wrong with his back, it had cleared up since he'd helped us out. Another person who'd been having problems with insomnia started sleeping like a baby, and the fourth person, who'd been on anti-depressants for years, suddenly started feeling *fine*. She stopped taking her medication, and hadn't suffered any setbacks.

Word of this got to the head of the Psychology Department, and he requested to see all our data. We were more than happy to show him—hell, we'd documented everything from the first minute we began—and he was impressed, so much so that he suggested we take the experiment to the next level.

One of the things Jenny had attempted was to use Cymatics as a way to treat mental illness—entraining misfired synapses in the brain to fall into a steady, predictable pattern. So what effect might genuine madness might have on the structure of things, and vice-versa?

The Psychology Director made arrangements for us to conduct the experiment on a handful of schizophrenics at the state mental hospital. I was amazed he was able to arrange all of this so quickly, but he pointed out that there was nothing about the experiment that put anyone in danger; it was a simple measurement of physiological reactions to auditory and visual data.

The only difference was that, this time, we'd be doing it with a dozen people simultaneously. The hospital had more than enough EKG and EEG machines to supply us.

So everything was arranged, and off we went.

The first part of the experiment went beautifully. The patients sat there and watched the screen and listened to the music—Steve's original composition, not the reaction recording—and then we made arrangements to come back in two days and play the results.

There was no deviation. Each of the twelve reaction pieces were the same kinds of tone poems that we'd gotten before, and just like the original batch of recordings, these twelve pieces, when played simultaneously, created a single melody. And just like the first series, there was that *chattering* on the periphery.

Steve had isolated the original chattering, but it was gibberish—a bunch of monosyllabic noises, like grunts or hums. This new series of noises was just more of the same, but then we overlapped the two sets of noises…and I suppose that was the moment we damned ourselves, because when combined, the two sets of noises formed a *chant*, some sort of…I don't know…incantation—Steve was the one who called that one. He said something about the rhythms and tonal phrasings matching those of Gregorian religious music led him to believe it was chant of some kind. Neither one of us recognized the language—assuming it *was* an actual language. We thought about taking it to the Language Department, but that would have delayed the second part of the experiment at the state hospital, so we just added that to our To Do list for afterward.

By this time, the two of us were the talk of the university. Even though the term wasn't over, we received notification that not only would we remain on scholarship, but would be receiving a small stipend to help continue our work—hell, the Bioacoustics Department even decided to resurrect the Cymatics program for the next term. We were stars.

A week later we went back to the state hospital to perform the second half of the experiment. Besides the original twelve patients, the state hospital director was present, as were two armed security guards and the head of the university's Psychology Department.

The patients' chairs were arranged in a half-circle in front of the large LCD screen. The hospital director and Psychology Department head sat in chairs a few feet off to the left of the group, and one security guard stood at each end of the half-circle of chairs. Steve and I were hunched over the equipment in a far corner of the room, a good ten feet away from everyone.

The lights were lowered, and we began the playback. Steve had made two master recordings; one of the patients' reactions, and one wherein their reactions were combined with those of the original test subjects. We'd programmed the system to play these back to back.

During the playback of the patients' reaction recording, Steve and I began to notice that the Fractal Visualization program wasn't behaving normally; instead of showing a cascading series of images, it was showing bits and pieces of the same image over and over, sometimes combining pieces, but more often just displaying a flash here, a section there. The patients themselves seemed utterly transfixed by it all, so we made a note and sat back to watch what would happen during the next playback.

The patients' reaction recording segued seamlessly into the combined recording, but this time, even though Steve had done nothing to amplify the chanting, the words could be clearly heard: *Iä-R'lyeh! Cthullhu fhtagn! Iä! Iä!*

We looked at one another. The chanting was the same volume as the music itself, and we had done nothing to alter the recording.

Iä-R'lyeh! Cthullhu fhtagn! Iä! Iä!

It didn't take long to figure out why. Many of the patients were moving in their chairs, rocking back and forth, and repeating the chant over and over.

Iä-R'lyeh! Cthullhu fhtagn! Iä! Iä!

I was watching the reactions of the hospital director and the head of the Psychology Department when I felt Steve's hand grip my forearm and squeeze. I looked at him, and he pointed toward the screen.

I don't know if I can find the words to describe the image I saw displayed there. It looked at first like some kind of huge squid with its writhing feelers whipping and curling all over the screen, but the more the music played and the louder the patients' chanting became, the image began to solidify.

It wasn't a squid, not exactly—whatever this thing was, it had the *head* of a squid. Its shoulders were dark and massive, and it was *reacting* to the chant and music. Saw something like a clawed hand press against the screen and almost laughed, it seemed so absurd.

But then the screen itself began to…and I know how this is going to sound…the screen began to bend and expand, almost as if it were melting outward.

Iä-R'lyeh! Cthullhu fhtagn! Iä! Iä!

And then it happened: a tentacle moved forward from the screen and out toward the patients. The air was suddenly filled with the stench of dampness and rot. Both Steve and I started choking as soon as the stink hit us, and I saw, for one brief moment, the tip of another tentacle push outward as the screen continued to expand.

Both security guards unholstered their weapons and began firing at the tentacle, but by then the second one was fully free and they… Christ, they never had a chance. Each of them were grabbed by a tentacle that wound around their torsos, lifted them from the ground, and began crushing them. They dropped their weapons as blood began fountaining from their mouths and by this time the hospital director was running for the alarm and the head of the Psychology Department was screaming for us to turn everything of, turn it off now, and we did, we yanked the cords and hit the switches *but the music continued*, it grew in volume and intensity as the screen kept expanding and more tentacles began slithering through, only now I could see the first few clawed fingers tearing through the scrim, and I realized that whatever this *thing* was, it was the size of a small mountain on its side of the screen, but when it emerged into our world, it easily tripled in mass and if it somehow managed to get all the way through….

I started to move—where I was going or what I was going to do, I had no idea, it just seemed to me that it was important that I *do something, anything* to ground myself, to get a hold on matters, to somehow come to grips with this…this *nightmare* that was unfolding before my eyes, so I began to move and my foot kicked against something solid and when I looked down I saw one of the security guard's guns and I grabbed it up and fired into the nearest tentacle, but it slammed me aside and grabbed the Psychology Department head while another took care of the hospital director, and within seconds there were four crushed, thrashing, bleeding bodies bouncing around in the air above our heads like marionettes and I couldn't move without having blood rained down on my face and in my eyes, and that's when I realized that the music and the chanting were coming from the patients themselves, many of whom had risen from their chairs and fallen to their knees, arms reaching upward, imploring, giving me my answer, telling me that, yes, all consciousness is connected as a primary wavefront phenomenon that allows us not only to resonate to such notes, but to play a few of our own back here and that there *was* a base wavefront to which all of them are connected, and

I would have been wrong calling that base God but not *a* god, because right here, right now, that god was pushing through the boundaries of perception to reclaim some part of the world over which it once must have ruled and, ohGod, God, *God*, there was no way to stop it, no way to send it back because the nested hierarchies of vibrational frequencies that had opened this doorway were no longer under the control of our machines, they were in the control of those kneeling before this god and howling *Iä-R'lyeh! Cthullhu fhtagn! Iä! Iä!,* and for a moment I was paralyzed with this knowledge, and then I saw Steve's broken, bleeding body dance across the air over my head and I did the only thing I *could* do, I scrambled on hands and knees to find the gun that I had dropped, and I found not only it but the other guard's gun, as well, and I ran to the front of the room and I began firing at each every one of their heads. Some of them looked at me before I killed them, and their eyes…ohgod, their confused, frightened eyes…there were in the grips of some form of rapture that was both euphoric and terrifying and they couldn't choose, they couldn't fight against it—maybe they didn't *want* to fight against it, I'll never know—but I killed them, I killed all of them, and with the death of each one some part of this thing, this god, this monster, this creature of rot and death and putrescence, recoiled back into the screen until it was done, until they all lay dead at my feet, and I faced the screen and I saw it *looking* at me, sitting very still, and I *felt* as much as heard its voice vibrate through my body.

You have shown me the way back, and here I will wait, for I will not have to wait long. Thank you for this music of bleak entrainment, this song that will very soon call me home.

I was in the process of removing the discs when the authorities arrived.

And that, as the saying goes, is that.

What? Yes, I know I was charged in all seventeen deaths, but I'm telling you for the record—for all the good it will do—that I only *purposefully* killed twelve people. Though I suppose, in a way, I did kill them all.

Now let me ask you something—*why* are you here? I mean, I've been locked up in here for one-third of my life and you're the first reporter to show up here since the initial circus right after it happened. What's going on that's made me the focus of interest all of a sudden?

They *what?*

Oh, dear God…who's got them? When were they found? Have they been played yet?

Listen to me—*they must never be played again*, do you understand? *Never*. Because that's what it's waiting for, what it's been listening for ever since that night. Please, *please*, tell whoever has them that those discs must *not* be—

—why are you calling for the doctors? There's no need to—

—hello, folks, look, yes, I got a little excited, but she's got to be made to understand that—oh, Christ, not with the needle again, wait, wait one second, *just give me ten fucking seconds and I'll*—

—ohgod—

—please tell them, *please*, I beg you…don't play the discs…never play them…because…if you do…he'll come home…

…feeling so tired now…so tired…

…he's still listening…he'll always be listening…

…sing him no songs, or the world will never sing again…. ▲

Walpurgis Eve

K. A. Opperman

The crickets chirp their plaintive tune
To charm the mystic afternoon,
While through the amber mist the moon
Gleams wanton, wild, and white.

The faeries dance their roundelays,
Glimpsed only by the vagrant gaze
That scans the florid sward, where haze
Of dreams enchants the sight.

When twilight falls the witches ride
Their brooms to sabbats far and wide,
Each one to be a devil's bride
And dance around the fire.

They skip around the sickly flames,
All naked, shrieking ancient names.
A goat-god, Master of the Games,
Foul offspring soon will sire.

Into the Mountains with Mother Old Growth

by Christian Riley

She drove like a woman heading to her husband's funeral, hit the dirt road off the main highway at a snail's pace then began limping over washboards, dragging their Subaru Outback into a canyon of ancient trees and countless ferns.

Kevin didn't mind the slow crawl up the hill, and to the trailhead. He was having second thoughts about his plan, though he had told himself that this would be the case. He had prepared for such mental detours, and promptly focused on the steps he would need to take to get through his first night.

"I still think you're crazy," Vanessa said. Her voice was a reed instrument and her eyes shimmered like wet glaciers, cold and blue. "What if you get lost?" The question was insignificant at this point, asked a dozen times already, amongst a host of other *What-ifs*.

"How am I going to get lost when there's a trail?"

"You don't have to be smart about it."

Half an hour later Vanessa edged the car up to the trailhead then put it in park. She left it running. Kevin knew his wife wasn't impressed with him, and that she was likely holding back a mouthful of obscenities. She had never understood his desire to spend two weeks alone, up there in the rugged mountains of northern Washington, and had taken the notion as a mild affront. Also, there was that horrific incident last year with that backpacker, Spencer Heathrow. Kevin thought that that might have weighed heavy on Vanessa's mind. No, she didn't understand his wild notions one bit, probably thought he was crazy. For her, a good time meant holding hands on the beach and watching the sunset. Or cuddling on the couch, sunk halfway into a bottle of Pinot blanc before the movie started.

"You just don't get what it means to be a man," Kevin said. "I've got instincts, you know? Kind of like an ancient calling." He climbed out of the car and retrieved his backpack from the trunk, slid into it. "Read Jack London's, *Call of the Wild.*"

Vanessa gave Kevin a defeated look, which softened his pride, because frankly he was scared shitless. Growing up in the suburbs of Portland marked him as a "city-boy" in all approximations, and he shivered at the thought of spending a single night alone, off the beaten path. He shivered at the thought of the very evening looming before him. Of course, he'd gone backpacking a few times with some chumps from college, but that was safety in numbers.

"I don't need to read any stinking book, Mr. Cooley." She had changed her tone, did that about-face she often did when confronted with the inevitable. Kevin smiled as his wife crashed over him then, arms wrapping him in a tight hug, whispering into his ear to be careful, that she loved him, and couldn't wait to see him again. But when Vanessa drove away, Kevin had never felt so alone in his life, and his smile fell from his face like the drop of a dead hand.

* * * *

The media had suggested the work of a serial killer, but the authorities were quick to caution that one such murder, however brutal and grotesque in quality, did not necessarily indicate the presence of a homicidal maniac roaming the Northern Cascades. They added that in all likelihood, the murder was simply a crime of passion brought on by a former acquaintance of Heathrow's.

Theories notwithstanding, the horrific incident oddly served as a catalyst for Kevin's decision to spend two weeks alone, backpacking in a similar area of northern Washington. As a high school English teacher, he was prone to frequent philosophical ruminations. He knew this about himself, and as such, was not surprised that the murder had played into his unrelenting internal battle. While his gut carried the weight of the primordial fears associated with being alone, in the outdoors, his mind often dissected the rational explanations to each of those fears. And there were many rationales to consider.

Take, for instance, the case of the dead backpacker. Albeit the authorities might have hit the nail on the head with the crime being passionate in nature, a possibility that occurred to Kevin was that Spencer had simply bushwhacked off the trail, then stumbled across marijuana farmers, or game poachers. Since Kevin had no intention of "bushwhacking," the minute quandary of getting beheaded and quartered while on vacation seemed irrelevant.

There were other problems though; such as becoming lost, breaking an ankle, or being attacked by a bear or mountain lion. But Kevin felt prepared for these concerns, and others like them. And while stewing over the various situations he could potentially face, Kevin reminded himself that "history" was the tome of evidence to look back at, on those nights when he sat alone near the fire, nothing but the wind and the trees, and the surrounding darkness. History had thousands of accounts where individuals had succumbed successfully to the call of the wild: Native Americans, fur trappers, miners, cowboys, survivalists, etcetera, and etcetera, and if they could do it, then why couldn't he? Logically, it seemed more than rational. It seemed obvious.

* * * *

The trail broke into a wall of earthy colors, reds and browns and every shade of green imaginable. Massive sequoias—trees bigger than life—stood so still. It baffled Kevin how something so big could be so quiet. He imagined every tree a poet, lost in thought, searching for that next perfect word. Serrated fern leaves reached along the trunks of these trees, or into the trail, brushing Kevin's legs as he walked by—the silence ever known to a forest this old, broken at last. It was peaceful, and Kevin briefly observed this…only because it was daylight.

The terrain will change, he told himself, just to keep his mind off the impending evening. It had been not fifteen minutes since he watched Vanessa drive away, and already his nerves of steel were scratching on glass. *The trail runs for eighty miles, so yeah, the terrain will change.*

He put his nose to the grindstone and increased his pace, figured to burn up some adrenaline. To reach the road Vanessa would pick him up at, he had to make roughly six miles a day, which was a breeze no matter how he cut it. And Kevin was in good shape. Eighty pounds of gear on his back and he hadn't yet broken sweat—which was good, since 'sweat kills' as the saying goes. Kevin had prepared for that also. His clothes were layered, and nothing cotton, not even his underwear. He had dropped several hundred dollars on some of the best name-brand items on the market: Smartwool Microweight T-Shirts, Terramar Thermasilk tops and bottoms, Dakota Grizzly convertible pants, Merrell Moab Ventilators—the works.

In Kevin's mind was a list of all the crap on his back, and it was a beautiful list if there ever was one. He found his extra clothes halfway down the page, between waterproof matches, and anti-fungal cream. He went through the list regularly, methodically, as it was a comforting exercise. (One that stood as a wedge as much as a crutch; and by two weeks, he hoped that wedge would dislodge itself, that he would find comfort with just being alone in the wilderness.)

Still, comfort was a ship on the horizon. Absently, Kevin reached down and tapped the can of bear spray on his hip. He had a K-bar knife also, strapped onto the side of his backpack. Small comforts, but not any real comfort; the kind he'd find lying in his own bed, next to Vanessa, her chestnut thigh angled over his abdomen. *Get your mind off them thoughts boy, back to the list—wool socks, first aid kit, hundred feet of parachute cord...*

Later, the trail opened into a meadow the size of three football fields. The terrain had changed already, into another picturesque backdrop. It looked like a photographer's wet dream. Kevin's thoughts instantly went to bear, or elk; potential encounters, both as equally prevalent and dangerous.

He glassed the meadow with the binoculars hanging from his neck, saw a couple of black-tailed deer grazing off to the right; they seemed comfortable enough. The grass stood knee-high, swayed steady from a slight breeze, and was spotted with pink lilies and purple hyacinths. Kevin caught the smell of oats, and damp earth, with a slight touch of botanic potpourri.

He took his time through the meadow, contemplating this and that, until his thoughts ran aground onto the topic of kids. Vanessa had been bugging him for months now. Her clock was ticking, ticking fast. The woman had recently changed, Kevin observed. She'd become more neurotic, started getting on him about those little messes he'd leave around the house. He thought this was called the "nesting phase" of pregnancy—even though she wasn't pregnant.

A dark blur off to his right clipped his thoughts. The flash of movement preceded a series of low thumping sounds. Kevin froze, turned his head, then spotted the last deer as it dashed into the tree line. He glassed the area again, found nothing but a few swaying branches. In the peaceful silence that followed, Kevin thought he heard his own heart beat.

* * * *

He went through his list half a dozen times, and it had been over an hour since he left the meadow, but the forest still appeared to be closing in around him. "Appeared" is a nebulous word though, often associated with the imagination. Kevin had read about this; along with the human psyche, and how it became unbridled from the jitters.

"Just part of the process," he said to himself, none too quietly. "There's a logical order to getting over my fear of being in the outdoors. Just have to work my way through it."

There was a placating effect to hearing his own voice, and he decided to run through his list another time, speaking aloud. He'd alert most animals, but for now, Kevin was fine with that, figured he'd see plenty of wildlife in the days to follow.

He started at the top of his list with *raingear*, and this got him past the next hour and to the next clearing, which was half the size of the previous one, but contained a small lily pond. Kevin looked up at the sun, raised a flat palm just below it, estimating how much time he had before things got dark. It was an old trick—fifteen minutes for every finger—and with trees this tall, he calculated two hours. He reasoned he would soon need to make camp, looked for a good place, and found one a half mile past the clearing.

It was an open area in the trees, beside a massive boulder. Kevin set his backpack in the dirt and scanned the area, looking for sign of bear. He proceeded to set up camp, keeping certain to make a lot of noise. He had a one-person bivvy tent, which he never really liked. It made him nervous, claustrophobic even: to be so close to the worries of the night, yet unable to see anything. He would have preferred a much larger tent, but that was unrealistic for backpacking. Sleeping out in the open was a possibility. He thought he might try that one night.

Before long, Kevin had everything squared away in his camp. He'd built a fire ring using granite knock-offs from the residing boulder, and collected plenty of dry wood from a fallen ponderosa. Soon, he had a roaring blaze going, and that did wonders to his psyche. Dinner was dehydrated stew, corn bread, and plum pie. All that was missing was a cold beer, and that got Kevin contemplating potential business opportunities, until the remaining twilight slipped off into the forest. After a series of three long yawns, he reluctantly crawled inside the bivvy, and into his sleeping bag. He clutched his bear spray in his right hand, and the K-bar in his left, listened to the crackle of the fire, and prayed he'd fall fast asleep.

* * * *

His nightmare contained Vanessa, with three strange, humanoid creatures, each dressed in gray lab coats and surgeon masks. Roughly, the creatures took turns peeling Vanessa out of her clothes, while, (and with considerable horror), she made quick work at theirs. Fully naked, they looked half-man, half-bear, with bald, leathery skin stretched taut, revealing boney frameworks. Their heads were gnarled and coarse, faces protruding into short snouts, bearing ragged canines. They never spoke, only made wet and labored guttural sounds. They led Vanessa through an exhaustive night of debauchery, and more than once, she groaned something about making babies.

The dream had come and gone throughout the night, in between Kevin's usual midnight piss in the dark, and several heart-stopping wake-ups, where he thought he had heard something big walking around his camp.

Morning came with nothing short of relief.

* * * *

After a good stretch, Kevin brought the fire back and made coffee. He sat on a rock, hands cupped around a steel mug for warmth, and inhaled deeply the aroma of dark roast, as he stared at the surrounding woods, the patches of blue sky, the cold dirt at his feet. The nightmare had stamped his morning with disturbing images; along with grim reminders, as he suddenly recalled how the media had reported Spencer Heathrow's fate: *...thoroughly disemboweled, roughly butchered, and stuffed unceremoniously into his backpack.*

Even so, Kevin had made it through his first night alone in the wilderness. The city-boy felt a slight surge of victory tumble down his spine. Thirteen more nights to go, and he was confident that he could do it.

After breakfast, Kevin released his bowels over a fallen log, broke camp, then languidly strolled down to the trail, working the stiffness of the previous day's hike out of his joints. It was then he regretted not packing some marijuana along for the journey.

To the east, snow-capped mountains rose into a steel-blue sky, brushed with brass and fire. Along the shoulders of a distant riverbank, groups of Whitebark Pine stood proud, like sentries of old, long and forgotten. The morning was both peaceful and lonely, yet around noon, suddenly, and unexpectedly, Kevin came across a man and woman at the side of the trail, sitting against the base of a sequoia. They were fellow backpackers, presently snacking on granola and dried plums.

"Hey there," greeted the man, cheerfully. He looked about Kevin's age, late twenties, and the woman a little younger. Her smile was inviting.

"Good afternoon," Kevin said, with vigor. He was thrilled to be in the company of other people again. "Isn't it awesome out here?"

"Sure is," replied the man. He had a lanky, athletic build, suggesting a familiarity to one or more of the activities of a triathlon. His face was relatively clean-shaven, save for ten inches of hair sprouted from his chin. A blue bandana wrapped tight across his forehead, fanning backward, marginally concealing a bushel's worth of short, stubby dreadlocks. "Been out here long?" he asked.

"Came out yesterday." Kevin slithered out of his pack, set it on the ground. He dug into the top pocket and pulled out a bag of cashews. "Staying for two weeks, though."

"Righteous," replied the woman.

They took an hour visiting, sharing anecdotes about backpacking, and other general topics. The man's name was Vance, and he worked at a bicycle shop outside Tacoma. A mountain biker on the semi-pro circuit, he was hoping a good finish in one more race might get him a sponsorship with Yeti Cycles.

His fiancé, Willow, worked customer service at a Trader Joe's. She had originally planned on beauty school, but the many chemicals associated with that occupation proved disconcerting. She was saving money to open a boutique, featuring all-natural products.

Kevin thought Willow would have little problem representing those products of her future store. Normally not one for dreadlocks on women, he observed a mild appreciation for the burgundy tendrils stretching to her waist. The locks were artfully festooned with what he soon learned to be maple beads and lavender-dyed hemp fiber. Willow's slim build and narrow facial features insinuated birdlike qualities, but the tone of her voice had Kevin thinking more along the lines of a cartoon caricature of a mouse. In a natural way, Kevin admitted, she was both cute, and provocative.

Heading the same direction, the three of them spent the remainder of the day hiking, pointing out wildlife, and philosophizing on the human condition as it related to nature. Later, around a fire, they had taken this topic (as well as others) into a more speculative realm, via the inducement of certain hallucinatory amplifications. (Vance's homegrown weed was stellar, Kevin declared, and with much gratitude.)

The evening trolled on into the small hours, and the mood eventually grew listless and heavy. Conversations whittled away, and despite the euphoric membrane surrounding Kevin, (thanks to the pot), he now felt like the proverbial third wheel. After a piss in the woods, he bid Vance and Willow goodnight, and crawled into his bivvy. He fell fast into a deep sleep, his last thought being that of his wife's face.

* * * *

They were gone in the morning. Their stuff was still there, but they were gone. A day-hike was the logical assumption, but it seemed to Kevin that the couple hadn't taken anything with them. They'd even left their water bottles. By late afternoon, when they still hadn't come back, and after Kevin had searched the general area more than once, called out their names numerous times, his nerves were having the best of him. *Where the hell were they?*

It was half-past two, and Kevin's stomach was mad with hunger. He sat on the ground near his tent, ate crackers and cheese, and pondered over the situation. He had hoped to get a few miles down the trail, but felt awkward to leave without saying goodbye to Vance and Willow. (Or, at this point, without resolving the question as to what had happened to the couple.)

After putting away his food, Kevin drank from his water bottle, when he then spotted a peculiar blemish high on the trunk of a nearby birch tree. The scaring appeared to be from the result of some sort of writing, and sat roughly fifteen feet high.

Curious, Kevin stood, walked to the base of the tree and looked up, studying the scabbed bark. It took less than a minute before he felt the cold finger run down his back, as he made out the words, MOTHER ~~SPENCER~~ WAS HERE.

* * * *

He decided to stick it out and wait at the camp, hoping Vance and Willow would eventually return; their arrival would release him from the anxious dread presently swinging an eight-pound hammer in his gut. He made piles of wood near the fire, enough to last until the morning, and pulled his sleeping roll out of the bivvy. If he got any sleep at all, it would be on the ground, free from the claustrophobic confines of the little tent.

His hands felt like wet tortillas, and as dusk slowly sucked away the light, it seemed to Kevin that the surrounding forest had come alive. Peripheral shadows moved, sounds occurred, the air *breathed.* He clutched his bear spray to his chest and walked circles around the fire, trying desperately to convince himself that it was all his imagination, and that Vance and Willow would return—*any minute now!* And up until he heard the great sound in the trees, Kevin had almost wholly convinced himself that yes, his mind *had* been playing tricks on him.

It came from back down the trail, a hundred yards or so: a mass rending of wood, deep churn of earth and rubble, accompanied by a cavernous groan lasting for several minutes. After, a gust of hot air rushed through the camp—the furnace blast—carrying with it a stifling stench of compost, and something else...*blood?*

Kevin's knees buckled, his mind dithered. Nothing rational about any of this, he was sure. There was something dreadful out there.

He moved fast. He packed his gear, all of it, pausing when finished. The night had fallen silent once again—*too silent*, he thought. He was reluctant to leave the fire, and, adding more wood, he crouched low, listening.

It was as if the night had drawn a long breath, then held it. The monotonous hiss and cracks from the burning wood were the only sounds. The surrounding forest stood as an ominous wall, black as the grave. Kevin's knuckles grew white over bear spray and the K-bar, and he swore to God this wasn't happening to him, swore to God he should have stayed home.

A sudden onset of continuous screaming pulled a jagged razor across his scalp. A shrieking noise in the distance, it was unerringly human, sounded male, and unremitting. Amidst the high-pitched wail, Kevin repeatedly heard the words *Help!*, *God!*, *Please, and No!*, mixed and combined as they were, into horrific variations. And it lasted all night. It moved throughout the forest, and it came and went, like a reoccurring nightmare, but the screaming lasted all night.

Sick with dread, Kevin crouched by the fire and trembled. Completely, physically, he shook with fear. Twice he vomited in the dirt, and almost soiled his pants after a particularly long and arduous wail, containing the phrase, *My God, please...no more, no more!* But he didn't dare move. To leave the fire meant to go into the darkness and join that which was producing the torment.

He was convinced it was Vance out there, screaming in pain, for mercy. Kevin thought about Willow: Was she too in hiding, her stomach clenched, nerves knotted, as she listened to her fiancé's blood-curdling throes?

It occurred to Kevin that a bear would have finished the job long ago, and a sick joke from the couple did not explain the prodigious noise he had heard earlier. *Whatever was causing all that horror wasn't natural.*

But his thoughts were transitory; thin moments of reduction stretched over an all-encompassing face of terror. Bear spray in hand, Kevin sat in the dark and waited for the light.

* * * *

When it came, it brought silence. The first shade of light was a pallid veil that smoothed over the sky and between the trees, and it brought with it the most unnerving calm. Kevin strapped his backpack on and headed out. He would go the other way, back to the trailhead, the dirt road, down through the canyon, the main highway. It was the shortest distance to any semblance of civilization, and he thought he could cover it by nightfall. Damn if he was going to stay another night in these woods.

He paced himself at a slow jog. He felt the efflux of adrenaline congregate above his knees, in his fingertips, below his eyes; electric, like the jitters from too much coffee. His bowels roiled from fear, and the urge to shit was both strong and often. As he imagined something cold and ugly staring from the trees, he decided to keep moving.

Minutes on the trail, and Kevin came across a gaping hole in the ground, as wide as a city bus, elongated like a mouth, a perimeter strewn with the detritus of earth and wood and other things; he saw broken bits of bone, scraps of curled flesh, knobs of blackened meat. He felt the sudden press of a chilled hand onto his abdomen. A damp odor of decay hung in the air, thick and foul, and it wormed its way into the back of Kevin's throat, sat there like a wet sponge. As he looked upon the grisly site, his mind went to the "great sound" from the night before. It was as if the forest had wrestled in labor, prospered, and Kevin was now observing the afterbirth.

An opalescent sheet dropped over his eyes, fogging his vision, his thoughts. At once, the world felt so heavy, even as he dropped his pack and hit the trail at a full sprint. He became acutely aware of the sound of his boots slapping against the ground, and the feral strain of his breathing. A sharp laugh came from the distance, and then Kevin stumbled, gouged his palms on gravel, tasted dirt.

He pushed up, rising against the invisible anvil fixed between his shoulders, and broke into another run. And he ran for days, so it seemed, his mind lost within that pearly veil, until at last, the spiral of his absence uncoiled with a vivid *snap!*

As it happened, Kevin found himself on the bank of a fast-flowing river: an afternoon sun riding treetops, birds skipping on branches, the scent of pine stirring in the breeze. Presently, he was staring at a large steelhead idling in the ebb behind a boulder, unsure as to the admiration he felt for the thing, why it made him weep so.

Something inside his gut whispered that the trail was forever gone. Nothing around him appeared remotely familiar, only thick woods hunched behind him. A map of scratches caked in dried blood covered his arms, and his face felt the sting of a hundred ants. Excrement soiled his clothes. He was missing a front tooth.

He saw her then, standing on the opposite bank. She had an uncanny resemblance to those monsters of his dream, some nights before, except her face was pie-shaped, less protruded. She stood over ten feet tall, bipedal, long arms extending to needle-like nails. Two sallow breasts hung low on her chest. Her hair was lank, her body gaunt, with smooth skin stretched paper-thin over an emaciated skeleton. Eyes, black as pitch, were smiling at Kevin.

Willow stood obediently at the creature's side, naked and bedraggled. She too was staring at Kevin, her face in mechanical motion of silent terror. Rivulets of blood painted her body, and she was stuck in a half-crouched position, as if broken somewhere on the inside.

With the effect of moving in slow motion, the creature lurched forward. She stomped a wide foot into the river and raised a pulsating hand, fingers pulling at dead air. Thin laughter accented her movement, as she approached Kevin.

His body recoiled. He heard his boots slip, felt the world spin, and the cold bite of the river through his pants. He met the creature's extended forearm with a raise of bear spray, his last memory being the sound of released pressure followed by a nebulous gray fog, a cloud of particles fouling the air. Then the darkness, and a length of time that could have been immeasurable, for all its obscurity.

* * * *

The forest around him stood tall and ancient, like a grove of sentinels that had all but devoured every tome of history known to man. Figuratively, Kevin had lost his sense of direction. His mind was only "half-there," accustomed now to being vaguely present; void of recollection, or thoughts of the future. He was distinctly aware, though, of the cold and wet ground beneath him. He was aware that he was sitting on the forest floor, his back against a tree. And he was aware that he was alive, albeit in considerable pain. The sounds of a highway fluctuated from afar, as if echoing the indeterminate lull of his breathing—an exercise that provoked a sting of fire and red-hot steel to surge between his ribs with each passing breath.

His backpack sat neatly across his legs, the top pocket splayed open, revealing a thicket of short, natty hair, scabbed flesh, and the corner of a blue bandana. Kevin stared at the ensemble; it seemed absurd that such a gruesome thing had found its way onto his "list" of gear, into his backpack. His thoughts receded and it was more of the cold and wet earth, a punch of wind carrying the smell of rain.

The sound of tires ambling over gravel made him look up. He felt a vast bewilderment to his surroundings—nothing ringing a bell, or striking a chord, other than the vehicle slowly approaching. It was a Subaru Outback.

He heard the squeal of brakes, the metallic acoustics of a door opening, and then, "Kevin?"

Shoes crossing dirt.

"Kevin? Is that you?"

The voice summoned a visceral sense of nostalgia inside him, followed immediately by anxious dread.

"My god, what happened?"

She was there, he knew...below the trees, cold and ugly, those smiling eyes.

He felt Vanessa's hands crawl over him, inspecting and caressing. They reached for the backpack, discovered its contents, and then his wife screamed; a shriek that was like the busting of a dam.

At once Kevin remembered everything: The day Mother took him in, at the river; the following days of servitude, crawling through endless mud and gore; the quiet nights, suckling mindlessly at her breasts; the hours she spent pulling Vance apart, Willow at her side; and the miles and miles of tunnels below.

Kevin hunched forward and retched, a spate of crimson bile and tangled hair splashing onto his lap, gagging the breath out of him. He felt the ground rumble, thought to tell Vanessa to run like the wind, to get in the car and stand on the pedal, but he knew it was too late. He had already heard the laughter. ▲

Sonnets of an Eldritch Bent

W. H. Pugmire

"The Hound"

I hear your ceaseless cry in tortured ear
As fate solidifies before my eye.
This Holland hill will be my moonlit bier
On which my mangled corpse will putrefy.
My breastbone is the bed of your icon,
Your amulet composed of antique jade;
That emblem formed in forgotten aeon,
That distant age of which you are one shade.
Ah, Sphinx of Hell, your grin is ever-wide,
It is the final doom I gaze upon.
No paltry god can stall my homicide,
No poetry from Necronomicon.
I take your savage kiss into my heart
As trenchant recompense for arcane art.

"The Haunter of the Dark"

Your lure was one that I could not resist,
And thus I staggered up your high plateau.
A sense of hazard could not be dismissed,
Its presence struck me as oppressive blow.
I crawled into your vaulted cellar space,
That place adorned with cobweb filigree.

I felt your darkness press against my face
As I crept forward through your vast debris.
I moved like dream through your colossal nave,
Where dying sunlight touched a blackened pane.
The paintings on your tainted windows gave
Me pause—the saints depicted were not sane.
I found the fabled stone that served as gate
For that which signaled my appalling fate.

"Pickman's Model"

Shew me the anatomy of fear,
Dazzle me with its morbid design.
Let me sense its presence drawing near;
Then, embracing it, I'll make it mine.
Ah, the physiology of fright—
How it can enthrall and captivate.
Teach me how to kiss the dreadful night,
Let your canvas serve as passion's gate.
I can smell the dim and antique time
That you've captured with your wizard art.
I'll descend into your pit of slime
Where humanity will fall apart,
Where I'll move in ghoulish dance and laugh
With the creature caught in photograph.

"The Outsider"

Oh, you are but a distant memory,
A phantom in some mental corridor,
A spectral and elusive visitor
I might have known in time of infancy.
Did you, in childhood's hour, caress my head,
And silence childhood's agony and gloom;
Or hold me in some dank and lonesome room
Where, wretchedly, I dwelt among the dead?
I call for you within the haunted place,
Although I cannot recollect your name.
I stagger 'neath black trees, confused and lame,
And try to catch in memory your face.
Perhaps you rest within the heap of bone
To which I stumble, dazed and doomed, alone.

The Grimlorn Under the Mountain

by James Aquilone

They were halfway up the mountain when Max fell into the yawning cave mouth.

He had been resting on a boulder as Richard went off to relieve himself. Max was happy for the break. Richard had been practically racing up the mountain. Max kept telling him to slow down, he was pushing a heart attack. But Richard was being his usual vindictive self. "Maybe if you stopped complaining you'd be able to keep up, princess," he would say, and run ahead.

Max knew saying yes to the "excursion" was a bad idea. But his brother was adamant and Max still felt guilty about that stupid loan.

He was ready to head back down the mountain, call it a day, when Richard returned from his bathroom break.

Max barely had time to stand before Richard charged and drove his shoulder into Max's midsection. Max stumbled back three steps, and then he went down. He expected to land on the ground, but instead he fell through the air.

Time froze. The world went silent.

Max must have cartwheeled, because he landed on his belly, hitting the water with a flat smack. It felt like he'd been whacked with a sledgehammer.

Somehow he fought his way back to the surface. It took a long moment before he caught his breath, looked up, and saw Richard leaning over a rough circular opening in the chamber's ceiling, like the oculus in a cathedral, at least thirty feet above him.

"Don't worry, Maxwell!" Richard's voice boomed through the chamber. "You'll be fine. You're always fine."

"What the hell are you talking about?" Max shouted. "You've got to get help, Richard! You've got to call someone!"

"Sorry, princess! It's a done deal." Richard shrugged—and then the hole closed like a pair of jaws.

Max was entombed in darkness. He screamed, "Richard! Richard! This isn't funny!" His voice thundered and rolled off into the cave's depths.

Did Richard just try to kill him? He was always a bit sadistic—that's how big brothers are made—but this was madness. *Let's go for a nice excursion in nature like when we were kids*, he said. Real nice.

Max treaded in the water, hoping Richard would appear above him, laugh, and throw down a rope. *Hey, little bro, just kidding, ha-ha-ha.* But then Max recalled Richard's smug expression when he charged and that casual shrug just before the cave mouth closed.

He began to swim.

He had traveled about twenty yards when he heard a voice calling his name.

"Max-*well*... Max-*well*..."

A finger of cold slid down his back.

"Max-*well*..."

The voice creaked like the opening of an ancient crypt door. It was as rough as glass scraped against stone, but Max was sure it was coming from a woman.

His hand landed on a narrow ledge just above the water line. His foot slipped off the slick rock four times before he was finally able to gain purchase and climb out of the water.

He stood against the rock wall, trembling. The sepulchral voice came again.

"*Max-wellllll...*"

He thought of answering, but his voice stuck in his throat. He reached for the cellphone in his back pocket. It wasn't there. It was most likely sitting at the bottom of the lake. He had a penlight attached to his keychain in his front pocket. That was still there—but it wouldn't light.

He crept forward, feeling along the rough wall, his heart thudding in his chest.

He wondered how the voice knew his name, but then he realized that Richard had shouted it before the cave mouth closed. *Don't worry, Maxwell! You'll be fine. You're always fine.* Those were their father's words. But they were always directed at Richard. The last time the old man told Richard he'd be fine was about a month ago, when he asked his father for a seven-thousand-dollar loan. Seems Richard, the big-shot lawyer, had gambling debts. It didn't help matters that the old man gave Max fifteen grand to open a bar just a year ago. "You're not Max," his father told Richard. "You're a hard worker. You don't need help. You'll be fine. End of discussion."

It wasn't the first time his father had said that, but it still stung. He guessed he deserved it. The bar closed in seven months. He should have known he wasn't cut out for entrepreneurship, or bars. Hell, he barely went to any before owning one. Richard took particular glee in his failure. Obviously his glee wasn't enough.

Max came to a passage. He stopped and removed the battery to the penlight, shook out the water, did his best to dry its insides. He put the battery back, and after a few attempts it emitted a weak brownish-yellow light.

The passage was narrow. Stalactites hung just above his head like demonic teeth. The ground was smooth and sloped slightly downward. He hesitated. Stumbling around a dark cave wasn't a great idea, unless you wanted to break your neck. The voice came again—Max-*well*, Max-*well*, Max-*well*—like the monotonous tolling of a church bell. There was something sad and horribly broken in that voice. He had to move.

To keep his mind off the voice as he crept through the cave system, he thought of all the unpleasant things he was going to do to Richard. Breaking his fucking nose was high up on the list.

* * * *

When the penlight died, Max took the opportunity to rest against a tall, thick column of stone. He had removed his wet shirt, rung it out, and done his best to dry it as he walked. Now he laid it out on a rock beside him. He removed his shoes and socks. His pants were still damp, but he left them on. He didn't like the idea of sitting naked in the dark.

The voice had disappeared soon after he entered the passage, but that made him feel only more uneasy. He was exhausted and terrified. He closed his eyes, rubbed his sore belly, and fought back tears. "You're going to be fine, Max," he whispered to himself, and laughed bitterly.

He didn't know how long he had been asleep, but when he opened his eyes he saw a dim light flickering to his left.

He got dressed and headed toward it. The light was coming from a slit in the rock wall. With a bit of effort, he was able to squeeze through the opening.

He stood on a narrow ledge that ringed a chamber that was as long as two football fields and almost as deep. Torches were scattered throughout the room, but the darkness was still winning the war. Thick, black shadows pooled around stalagmites clustered in the center of the chamber. They rose up, crooked and lumpy, disappearing into the darkness. The rest of the room was filled with boulders and mounds covered in a wet, pale-pink sheen that reminded Max of a movie alien's skin.

To his right, a steep slope led to the chamber floor.

When he was midway down it, a small figure slid out from behind one of the stalagmites.

He froze.

Torchlight danced over the creature's—the woman's?—shriveled and sunken face. Her hair, white as chalk, hung stiffly to the ground. Thin black veins stood out against her pale skin like cracks in marble.

"Max-well, you are finally here," the thing said in that horror-show voice he had heard earlier. She smiled to reveal small, jagged teeth. "Come closer, and let her see you better. The Grimlorn is happy now." She beckoned him with her hand.

He didn't move.

"Are you alone here?" he asked, his voice quavering. "Are there any others?"

Max looked around. Broken bowls and dishes, strips of cloth, and what looked like cheap jewelry littered the ground. He didn't see anyone else, but that didn't mean they weren't lurking in the shadows.

"There is only the Grimlorn. She is alone. For so long."

"Is that you? Are you the Grimlorn?"

"The Grimlorn Under the Mountain," she said, as if it were common knowledge. She stepped forward, squinted. "You are a handsome one, aren't you? What a pretty, pretty boy. Come, sit down."

Max thought of bolting back up the slope. But his penlight was dead and he knew the chances of finding a way out in the dark were slim. Reluctantly he made his way down to the chamber floor and sat on a flat boulder as far away from the Grimlorn as possible. He smelled meat boiling and then he noticed a bubbling pot behind the strange woman.

"You must be hungry," she said.

She squatted, reached under her dress, which was a patchwork of filthy and torn cloth that hung past her feet, and pulled out a small wooden bowl. She hobbled over to the pot and dipped the bowl into it. She returned, holding out the steaming contents.

Max realized, then, he was hungry—but not that hungry.

"Thanks," he said, "but I don't plan to stay. How do I get out of here?"

"The Grimlorn made it for you, *herself*," she said, and handed him the bowl, which was filled with fat lumps of meat covered in a dark brown goo. He held it in his lap.

The Grimlorn squatted in front of Max. "A pretty thing you are," she mumbled.

Max noticed a filthy cloth sack hanging from her side. But he didn't get a good look at it, because she suddenly twisted her body away from him.

She nodded expectantly, reached out toward the bowl. Her fingers were long and withered. Spidery veins crisscrossed her palms. "Eat," she said.

Max smiled. "Can you help me get back to the surface?"

"Eat. You will enjoy it. It is good. Do not let its appearance fool you. Please. Trust the Grimlorn." She watched him with tiny pink eyes.

No matter what she said, there was no way he was going to eat that slop. He saw where the bowl came from. He didn't want to know where she got the food. The best course of action, Max figured, was to ignore her.

He put the bowl on the ground.

The Grimlorn's eyes screwed shut and she began to sob. Then she fell onto the ground, rolling back and forth, like a petulant child throwing a fit.

"Are you okay?" Max asked, but the Grimlorn only moaned and writhed in reply.

Max had enough weirdness. He rose, grabbed a torch, and headed up the slope.

"You will be happy here!" the creature wailed as Max slipped out of the chamber. "Please! Trust the Grimlorn!"

* * * *

Max worked his way through the numerous passages and tunnels and chambers for hours. Several times he fell, scraping his hands and knees. Once he almost tumbled down a narrow chasm. He found columns of stone as tall as skyscrapers and a chamber filled with phosphorescent rock. He tried backtracking to the lake, but he couldn't find it.

Then, when he was exhausted and sure he was utterly lost, he found himself back in the Grimlorn's chamber.

She awoke with a start.

"Max-well! Max-well!" she said, sitting up. "You have returned!"

"Is there any way back to the surface?" Max asked, dejected.

"Out?" she said after a long silence, as if the idea were foreign to her. "There is no way out, Max-well. The Grimlorn should know. She has been here a long time."

"There must be. If we both got in, we can get out."

The Grimlorn fell silent again, staring into his eyes dreamily, as if she were trying to look into his brain. Suddenly she let out a sharp laugh.

"What?" Max asked, momentarily self-conscious.

"What beautiful teeth you have," she said. Max rubbed the tops of his thighs. "The Grimlorn has been here a long time. And she has been waiting."

"What about the cave mouth I came through?"

"It does not exist, not any longer. Perhaps another day, long from now, another will appear. But by then, you will not want to leave. Even if you did, no one will help you out. You belong here. With me."

"I belong getting drunk in my apartment, not in this hellhole," Maxwell said, and sat on the ground.

"You will be happy here. The Grimlorn would not have made the bargain if she thought otherwise."

Max's body clenched with anger. *It's a done deal.* "You made some deal with my brother Richard."

It wasn't a question, but she nodded. "A mouth opened one day and there he was looking down. But the Grimlorn did not ask him to help her out of the mountain. She asked for a husband."

Max ran his hand through his hair. "But it was a bargain. What could you give Richard?"

"Nothing good. It wasn't happiness—that the Grimlorn can assure you. He asked for riches, material possessions. Meaningless and trivial things. The Grimlorn got the better part of the bargain." She giggled. It sounded like water boiling in a cauldron.

"You were able to give him those things?" Max asked.

"He will come into them, yes."

The old man was right. Richard would be fine. The schemer found a way to get his money.

"You have magical powers, but you can't get yourself or me out of here?"

"There are rules. There are always rules, Max-well. Down here the Grimlorn can only give birth to pots and pans, occasionally food, trinkets. The Grimlorn gets only what she needs, nothing more, nothing less. The Grimlorn can make you a nice bracelet."

"Thanks, but that's not going to help either one of us get out of here."

"Max-well, the Grimlorn doesn't want to leave, this is where she belongs. You will not want to leave either, once you settle in. This is *our* home. We will make it beautiful."

Max leaned back and closed his eyes. At some point he fell asleep.

* * * *

Max awoke to the smell of roasting meat.

"Breakfast!" the Grimlorn announced as she pulled the skewered rats off the fire. Then she reached under her filthy dress and pulled out a ceramic plate. She placed the rats—at least Max thought they were rats—on the plate and handed it to him.

Max was starving, but he couldn't bring himself to eat her food. He didn't want anything from this creature. Eating it would only be an acceptance of his fate.

The Grimlorn sat beside him, waiting.

Max said, "Give me a minute. I can't eat first thing in the morning." He put the plate on the ground. He waited, but she didn't throw a fit. She bought it. He planned to dispose of the food when he got a chance and make her think he ate it.

Then, without a word, the Grimlorn dropped her head onto his lap.

"What the hell!" Max shrieked, and tried to scuttle back. But she kept her head firmly in his lap. Insects crawled in the matted strands of her hair.

"Max-well, we will be happy here," she said, lifting her head slightly.

Max shoved her harder than he meant to; it was like pushing a bag of dry leaves. She let out a soft cry when she hit the ground.

"What's with you?" he shouted. "There are—*things*—in your hair!"

"We can be happy," she said, tears welling up in her red-rimmed eyes.

"Please, stop saying that. Happiness isn't eating rats in a cave with a crazy old hermit. Trust *me*. I used to have a life up there. A pretty nice life."

That wasn't true. Most nights Max had to drink himself to sleep. During the day he avoided social contact whenever he could, rarely going out. He had zero friends. He never picked up the phone when his father called. The old man would only lay into him about the bar going bust or whatever else he could think up. That was one of the reasons he couldn't get out of going hiking with Richard. He knew Max had nothing else going on. He'd always say, "You have to stop hiding from the world, kid. Get out there, bust a few heads." God, he hated Richard.

The Grimlorn burst into tears. Her body heaved and then she began rolling on the ground.

Max ignored the tantrum. "How long have you been down here?" he demanded.

After about a minute, she sat up. "The Grimlorn doesn't know."

"How did you come to be here?"

"The Grimlorn cannot remember. It has been too long." She shook her head. "This is where she belongs."

Max gave up and searched, again, for a passage to the surface. Sooner than he would have liked, he was back in the Grimlorn's chamber.

* * * *

It was the same routine every day: The Grimlorn would cook a nasty-looking meal, Max would find an excuse not to eat it, and then given the opportunity she would drop her head in his lap. She never told him why she did that, and Max was beyond caring about her motives.

She wouldn't tell him about the sack that hung on her side, either. "Now that is none of your business, Max-well," she said through gritted teeth. "A woman has a right to *some* privacy."

"Is there something inside that could help us get out?"

"There is no way out. The Grimlorn told you that already."

There was little point in talking to her. She always gave the same answers.

"Why don't you give birth to a pick axe?" Max said. "Then I'll get us out of here."

"The Grimlorn gets what she needs, nothing more, nothing less."

And the Grimlorn got him, didn't she? She had some weird magical power, though Max didn't understand how it worked. She would simply reach under her dress and pull things out. Whenever he asked her about it, she would only say she had given "birth" to it. Did she give birth to whatever was in the sack? Why was she hiding it? Why did she get so angry when he talked about it?

Whatever was inside was important. It meant something. If he wanted to escape, Max was sure he'd need whatever was in that bag.

* * * *

"Are you happy, Max-well?"

Max was done fighting. If the Grimlorn wanted a husband, he would give her one. "Of course," he said.

"The Grimlorn does not lie. This place is not so terrible once you learn how to see in the dark. If you trust the Grimlorn, we will have a beautiful home together."

Over the next few days, Max continued to speak lovingly to the Grimlorn. He laughed with her, teased her. He lied about enjoying her cooking (though he continued to dump it down a chasm when she wasn't looking); she liked that especially, grinning and laughing like a little girl. At those times, Max almost enjoyed her company. He even had her make him a bracelet—a brown leather strap studded with tiny metal chips. She was delighted. He would pet her hand, hug her, get her used to the idea of him touching her. That was key.

But Max drew the line when she would place her filthy head in his lap, which she did every chance she got. He would push her away as always, and she would throw a fit.

One night, as she slept, snoring like a buzz saw, Max sidled up to her, held her in his arms—it felt as if he were hugging a bale of hay—and he gently slipped the sack off her belt. She went on snoring as Max grabbed a torch and sneaked out of the chamber.

When he was safely in one of the smaller rooms, he wedged the torch into a niche in the wall and opened the bag. Inside was a heart.

He didn't know what he'd expected to find. An amulet, maybe. A ring. A magical wand.

He held up the shriveled, desiccated organ. Soon after the heart began to pulse, the Grimlorn's voice erupted in one of the passages.

"Max-well? Max-well?" she was shouting. But soon she was screeching, "My heart! You stole my heart!"

There was something terrible about the way the black heart felt in his hand. It felt obscene, like a dead thing that didn't know it was dead. He wanted to tear it apart, stomp on it, destroy it. Would that kill her? If she died, would that free him? Is that what he needed to do?

He heard her feet slapping against the stony ground. And then she was in the chamber.

"Max-well, what are you doing? Give me the Grimlorn's heart!"

Max held the vile thing above his head. "Don't come any closer. I'll rip it to pieces."

The Grimlorn shrank back in terror. "Don't" was all she managed to say.

The heart was as dry and rough as sandpaper.

"This is what's holding me here, isn't it?"

"No, Max-well. The Grimlorn is not holding you here, nor is her heart. She and you are both trapped here. Why not make the best of it?"

"Best of it? You're insane. Look around you. This is hell. I think if I destroy your heart, it will kill you and then you won't have any power over me."

"Please, Max-well, give it back and we can be happy. It is up to you."

"Stop it! Stop saying that. I'll never be happy here. No one could be happy here. Look at you—you are a monster! This is a nightmare."

The heart swelled.

He could tear the heart like a sheet of paper—it had little weight to it—and put her out of her misery. It would be an easy thing to do. And even if killing her didn't release him, at least he wouldn't have to spend eternity with this mad woman.

Max's own heart beat wildly as he watched the Grimlorn standing before him, her pink eyes wet. She rocked back and forth and seemed to have shrunk to half her size. What if she was telling the truth? What if it was the mountain and she was just another victim?

For a long moment Max didn't move. Then with a sigh, he tossed the heart on the ground. "Take the damned thing!" he said, and fell back against the cave wall. He slid to the ground.

The Grimlorn picked up the heart, which was now flopping and twitching like a fish out of water.

"The Grimlorn loved you." Max could hear the sorrow in her voice. It sounded as if something inside her were breaking. "She gave you many opportunities, but you were a fool."

A glimmer of light flashed behind her eyes. She tilted her head straight back and dropped the wagging heart into her open mouth. Her throat bulged momentarily, like a bullfrog's, and then she gulped it down.

Her crooked and bent form straightened. She grew, as if something were filling her up. Her pale face reddened, as did her hair. Her pink eyes turned emerald.

She stood over Max, no longer the Grimlorn.

"But—"

"Does my appearance please you now, Max-well?"

Her skin burned bright as a torch, her eyes glowed with life. Her voice was as smooth as honey.

Suddenly her face contorted into a mask of terror. "It hurts, Max-well, my heart. That is why I kept it in my sack." She convulsed and doubled over but quickly righted herself. "You could have had my heart without stealing it. You could have made it not hurt. You only needed to see."

"I don't understand."

"Ignorance, Maxwell, is not bliss."

As Max tried to stand, her hand shot out, her sharp fingernails impaling his chest, and he fell back. He felt his flesh tear, his ribs separate and crack. It happened so fast, there was no pain, just a burning emptiness.

"What did you do?" he said. "Why don't I feel anything?"

The woman held up his still-beating heart. Unlike her shriveled, black heart, his was engorged with dark red blood.

"It only hurts when the heart is inside your body." She shuddered as if an Arctic wind had blown over her. "It's one of the many mysteries of the lonely mountain. I've given up trying to understand it. But there are rules. Follow them and you are rewarded. Don't and...well, I gave you plenty of chances."

Max held up his hand and gasped in horror. It had turned white as marble. He held up his other hand and it too was white. He watched as thin, black lines appeared just below the surface of his skin.

"What's happening to me?"

"It doesn't matter. It won't be long."

"Please, I just want to go home."

"You did not follow the rules, Max-well. If only you had learned how to see in the dark, but you saw only the shadows. You saw only a prison, not the possibilities. You saw only ugliness, and ugliness was returned to you. You could have been happy here, you could have had a kingdom and a queen. We could have shared it all. But it is clear now. You are not husband material."

And with that, she bit into his fat, red heart. Steaming blood filled her mouth and dripped down her chin. She tore and swallowed, tore and swallowed. Then, Max felt pain. He howled with each bite, fell to his knees, and held his hands over the hole where his heart had been.

With the last bite, a terrible silence spread throughout the cave.

* * * *

The Grimlorn didn't know what fraction of infinity had passed before she found herself back in the dark water. Time passed oddly under the mountain, if at all. Spears of golden light pierced the darkness from above. When her eyes adjusted to the glare, she saw a curious face looking down.

Finally, she thought.

"I am the Grimlorn Under the Mountain," she announced. "Send me down a husband and I will lavish you with riches beyond your wildest imagination."

The face lingered for a moment, and then disappeared.

She felt the nits multiplying in her hair, but she didn't pick them out herself. That was against the rules.

As she waited, she thought: Soon the Grimlorn will have a husband or she will have his heart. Either way, she would be happy, she would make the best of it. ▲

Dolls
by Paul Dale Anderson

Lizza was a living doll. Everyone who saw her said she looked absolutely picture-perfect. Her chubby little cheeks were delightfully pink, her button nose slightly upturned, her blonde hair long and curly, her eyes brilliantly blue. Lizza was seven years old when she killed her first human.

Lizza's mother carefully taught her. Lizza had accompanied mother on hundreds of hunting trips over the years and carefully watched as mother searched out women who were exactly right. Like Goldilocks, mother rejected those too big or too small, too young or too old. If a woman wasn't just right, she wouldn't do at all.

"Outer beauty is important," mother taught, "but inner beauty is essential. How do you know, Lizza, if a woman has inner beauty?"

"Her eyes?"

"What about her eyes?"

"They're alive?"

"Exactly. Eyes are the windows to the soul. If the eyes are alive, the soul is alive. Never, ever touch a dead soul, Lizza. A dead soul will rot you from the inside out."

Killing humans was easy, but extracting life's essence from a live person could be quite complicated. Mother had always demonstrated what to do while Lizza watched. Today was Lizza's turn to do while mother watched.

Mother looked like a living doll, too, except mother was all grown and appeared perhaps twenty years older than Lizza. But mother still looked so young and beautiful and picture-perfect, she could easily model for fashion magazines like *Vogue* or *WWD*. Mother remained young and beautiful through several centuries because mother was careful to feed only on the youngest and most beautiful of donors. "You are what you eat," mother always said, and Lizza could see it was true.

Mother had created Lizza to attract appropriate donors. When Lizza was little, women would approach Lizza to "Ooooo" and "Ahhhhhhh" and make funny faces and try to get Lizza to smile for them. Women were such suckers for babies. But even now, when Lizza was seven and no longer an infant, women often stopped to chat when they saw such a beautiful child. Lizza would smile and search their eyes for inner beauty. When she found a live one, Lizza would look to mother for approval. If mother shook her head from side to side, Lizza turned her attention away and the woman was left unharmed with no memory of seeing Lizza or her mother ever.

Ordinary people seldom saw what they didn't expect to see. No one could see a witch or her doll unless the witch willed it, and most people walked past mother and Lizza on the street or in shopping malls or lounging on park benches without noticing them at all. But when a young and beautiful woman approached, Lizza and her mother allowed themselves to appear. And when the woman saw Lizza, she felt compelled to come even closer, to reach out and touch the child's perfect hair, to stare into unblinking blue eyes until mother, or now Lizza, captured the woman's soul.

If other people passed by, those people saw nothing. Not only were Lizza and mother invisible to ordinary eyes, once a woman wandered within mother's sphere of influence, the donor disappeared from ordinary sight, too. Lizza or mother could do anything they wanted, and no one would know.

When young and beautiful women disappeared, authorities naturally assumed the woman had been abducted by a sexual predator. Nothing could be further from the truth. Witches and their dolls, like angels, were asexual. When a witch wanted a child, she made a doll. Mother had molded Lizza herself, and mother had taken eyes and hair from women who were alive and gave them to Lizza. Instead of nursing Lizza on breast milk, mother had nourished Lizza with the milk of human kindness stolen from unsuspecting souls.

Mother herself had been exquisitely crafted centuries ago in Germany by an ancient witch who had taught mother many secrets. After mother grew up, mother's mother crafted a new baby doll to attract donors and mother was forced to leave Germany because there weren't enough pure souls in all of Germany to feed three indefinitely. Mother went first to Vienna, then Paris, and eventually mother moved to England.

Mother had very nearly been incinerated when a buzz bomb exploded and scorched her porcelain-complected doll-flesh and human-like hair during the London blitz. Mother fled England for America. Mother's scars eventually healed, though it took years.

Mother said dolls could live forever unless destroyed by fire. In order to remain young and alive, however, dolls needed to feed at least once each week. Dolls had no souls and no life essence of their own, so they depended entirely on stealing the life-force of humans. If dolls didn't feed, they'd shrivel up and waste away. After seven days without ingesting a fresh soul, dolls became lifeless pieces of clay.

Mother had kept Lizza well-fed as a child, but now it was time for seven-year-old Lizza to learn to feed herself. As Lizza grew, she needed to devour more life-essence than what mother could comfortably share without starving herself. Someday, Lizza would grow up completely and have to move far away when mother made a new doll-baby to take Lizza's place. Lizza begged mother to teach her how to craft a doll of her own; mother promised Lizza she would as soon as Lizza was old enough to grasp all the facts of life.

Today mother had brought Lizza to Victoria's Secret in the shopping mall where a constant parade of young and beautiful women sauntered by. Lizza could pick and choose. Women with breast augmentation were instantly rejected as being too vain. Mother said dyed hair was okay because practically everyone dyed her hair these days. Tattoos were questionable. Nose jobs were a no-no. Lizza looked into the eyes of dozens of women but none seemed acceptable. They may look beautiful on the outside, but inside they were a mass of seething emotions, a nest of poisonous vipers. Their souls were vile and corrupted with vanity.

What would happen if Lizza found no suitable donor? Would she shrivel up and die? Lizza didn't want to die. Lizza had seen how humans shriveled up when mother absorbed their life essences. First their skin wrinkled, then their bones fractured, and finally their blood boiled. Then their mortal shells simply folded in on themselves and faded to dust. Like soda slowly sipped through a plastic straw, their life-force gradually diminished until the container was drained. When the container was completely empty, it imploded.

Because each time Lizza fed she acquired all the memories, hopes, aspirations, and dreads of the donor, Lizza had to be very selective. "You are what you eat," mother said, and it was so very true. Lizza became a combination of all of the essences she absorbed.

If a human donor were truly beautiful inside as well as out, Lizza felt beautiful and strong. Occasionally, when pickings were poor and mother had to settle for less than perfection, Lizza felt consumed with doubt and despair. Why weren't all women created equal? Why were some women happy and others sad? Why were some women vigorous and others listless? Why did some women seem so full of love and others soiled with jealousy and hate?

At seven, Lizza found it impossible to understand concepts like love and hate. Lizza supposed she loved her mother because mother provided food and shelter and taught Lizza things. Most of the women Lizza had absorbed loved their own mothers when they were children, but when they grew up they felt ambivalent about their mothers. Sometimes they loved their mothers, and sometimes they hated them. How could anyone hate her own mother?

Finally, an acceptable female donor looked into Lizza's eyes. Mother nodded a go-ahead, and Lizza pounced. Lizza's eyes drilled into the eyes of the donor, entered the donor's brain, and devoured the pineal gland. Without the pineal, all light in the woman's eyes went out, human flesh began immediately to shrivel, and everything the woman was—her essence—left her body and entered Lizza's. It took ten minutes for the transfer to complete.

Lizza was ecstatic. She had made her first kill, gorged herself on the emotions of the donor, and insured she would live another week. She was proud of her accomplishment, and mother seemed proud, too.

After mother fed on a donor of her own, mother and daughter returned home. They lived in an expensive third-floor apartment on the near west side of downtown. The woman who rented the apartment—a soul of questionable character—never knew Lizza and mother were there. Lizza and mother slept in a spare bedroom. Sometimes mother borrowed the woman's clothes because they were the same size. Sometimes mother and Lizza shopped in department stores for clothes of their own. No one saw them walk out with arms full of clothes—dresses and undergarments and even jewelry—nor did their images ever appear on security cameras. No one could see a witch unless the witch wanted to be seen.

Before the week was up, Lizza had to hunt again. This time mother chose a public park that provided a playground for kids. Lizza watched other children play on the teeter-totter and monkey bars and go up and down the big metal slide. Lizza thought it looked like fun and wished she could join them, but she knew playing with children was impossible. Dolls didn't play well with others.

Once, when Lizza was only four or five and mother was otherwise preoccupied, Lizza had revealed herself to a group of children in hopes of making friends. Somehow the children had instantly recognized Lizza as an outsider—someone not exactly like them and potentially dangerous—and they had called her hateful names. Some of the boys and even one of the girls had picked up stones and hurled them at Lizza, chasing her away. Lizza learned a painful lesson that day, and she never again revealed herself to children.

Lizza wanted desperately to understand why she had been rejected. She had delved into the memories of donors and searched for reasons, but none of the reasons she discovered made sense to her. Mother explained that the life essence of a child was decidedly different than an adult's. Children were not acceptable donors because children didn't yet know how to give. Giving was learned behavior, and children had much to learn before their souls matured. Immature souls were as poisonous as dead souls.

Men, too, made unacceptable donors. The life essence of a male was seldom nourishing and ofttimes destructive. Mother warned Lizza to stay away from men.

Life essence was a mystery. Lizza knew that humans were born with souls that possessed life essence. Witches and dolls had no souls and possessed no life essence of their own. So witches and dolls fed on the pineal gland—the seat of the human soul—to consume the life essences of donors. Memories, hopes, aspirations, and fears were part of the life essence and transferred. But the donor's soul itself did not transfer. A doll had no soul of her own and could never hope to acquire one.

What happened to the human soul when a doll stole the human's life essence away? Did the soul shrivel and die like the flesh?

Lizza had never wondered about such things before today. She had always accepted things exactly as they were. It was a given that humans existed, witches existed, dolls existed. It was a given that humans had souls and dolls did not. It was a given that witches and dolls could see humans, but humans could not see witches nor their dolls unless either the witch or doll willed it. That was the way the world worked.

It was also a given that witches and dolls fed on the life essences of humans as humans fed on the life essences of cattle, sheep, and pigs. All living things had to feed on other living things to stay alive. Lizza had never questioned why. It was simply the way things were. Mother had told her so, and Lizza never doubted mother.

Did cows and pigs have souls? They had life essence. Why would cows and pigs have souls when dolls didn't? And what was a soul anyway?

Lizza knew from her own experience that no two souls were exactly alike because each human soul had affected its life essence differently. Some souls were beautiful, and some not so beautiful. Lizza and mother remained beautiful because they fed off the life-essence of the most beautiful souls they could find.

Lizza looked at each of the young mothers who had brought their kids to this playground. Lizza knew to instantly reject women who talked to other women or talked on the telephone instead of watching their children. What Lizza wanted was a woman who demonstrated she loved her children more than she loved herself. Surely, there must be at least one.

Morning turned to afternoon, and dozens of women came and went. A few of the women came close, but they weren't perfect. Mother left to hunt for her own donor elsewhere, leaving Lizza entirely on her own for the first time ever.

Suddenly, Lizza was scared. What if she didn't find a suitable donor? Mother had waited until the week was nearly up to hunt. Lizza could feel her own skin already wrinkling. Or was that merely her imagination? How long before the last of the life energy she had absorbed a week ago ran out? Did she have hours or only minutes left?

There was so much Lizza didn't know and mother never told her. Or, perhaps, mother had told her but Lizza hadn't listened. It didn't seem so life-and-death important before when mother did all the hunting. Mother had always shared donations generously, giving Lizza as much as, if not more than, mother kept for herself. Mother was a good mother, not like the women Lizza saw today in the park.

You are what you eat. And if you don't eat, you die. That was a given. Life essence got used up and had to be replaced. Lizza knew she was almost out of time. She had to choose a donor while she still had the strength.

Lizza revealed herself to the nearest woman, a barely acceptable-looking frumpy thirty-year old, with uncombed hair who entered the park with a rambunctious three year-old son in tow and a colicky infant she pushed ahead of her in an old beat-up stroller, what Lizza's mother called a "pram" or a "baby buggy." Lizza had to work harder than ever to capture the woman's attention. The boy was being absolutely impossible, screaming and yelling. He tore free of his mother's hand, ran to a swing, and demanded his mother come push him. His mother tried hard to ignore him. The woman looked totally drained. When Lizza made eye contact, she saw the empty stare of a dead soul. Lizza reacted as if burned. She immediately pulled back and faded from sight.

Was there time to find another donor? The park was nearly empty except for five older boys who had stopped by the park on their way home from school to climb the monkey bars. Long sinister shadows had crept across the playground as afternoon faded to evening. It was getting late and mother hadn't returned yet. Mother had been gone a long time. Wasn't mother ever coming back?

Lizza began to cry. She didn't want to die.

"Oh, shut up!" the woman told her. Emotions depleted what little remained of week-old life force Lizza had left and made Lizza visible to human perception. How could Lizza have been so stupid to let her emotions run wild?

In desperation, Lizza fed on the fetid life force of the dead soul. Negative emotions instantly flooded Lizza from head to foot, filling her with fear and hate, shame and anger. Not only did Lizza now hate all humans, she hated life itself. She wanted to end all life, including her own and her children's lives. She had absorbed, Lizza realized too late, the thoughts and feelings of the hateful woman whose life-essence Lizza had just consumed.

Horrid thoughts occupied Lizza's mind. Lizza felt a need to strangle the obnoxious boy who was screaming even louder now that he could no longer see his mother anywhere in the park. Killing humans by stealing their life essences to prolong one's own life was necessary, but killing them simply to shut them up was something else entirely. Lizza was appalled by what happened next, but she couldn't stop herself. It was as if someone else's mind had taken complete control of Lizza's body, and Lizza no longer had a say in the matter.

Did those tiny seven-year-old fingers that tightened around the screaming boy's bony neck belong to a stranger? What about the two petite hands that pressed a pink blanket tightly against the infant's mouth and nose to stifle her incessant whimpers?

Lizza was careful not to allow others to see as her hands next picked up a sharp rock. She approached a group of five older boys on the monkey bars—she recognized them as the same neighborhood boys she had once revealed herself to and who had chased her away with rocks—and pounded each of them about the head and face until their heads split open like ripe melons. Four of the boys never knew what hit them. They were dead before they fell to the ground. The fifth boy—although he could see neither Lizza nor the rock she held in both hands—realized something was terribly wrong when each of his four companions fell, one at a time, to the ground, blood gushing from their faces and jagged-edged cracks in their skulls exposing their brains. The fifth boy tried to run. Lizza pounced and smashed his pudgy face in with the rock. She didn't stop pounding his face and head until his facial features turned into what looked like a pile of regurgitated lasagna.

Lizza felt she could do whatever she wanted, because no one saw a witch or her doll unless the witch or doll willed it. For the first time in her life—both her own life and the life of whomever was now inside of her—she felt powerful. And she found she liked the feeling.

Lizza was covered in blood, her cute pink dress ruined, but it didn't matter. Lizza knew where to find new dresses that were hers for the taking. She could walk into any store in town and walk out with whatever she wanted and no one would ever know.

Nor would anyone know that Lizza was no longer beautiful and no longer a child. No human would see the wrinkled and rotting flesh, the jagged nails, the broken teeth, the stringy grey hair that fell out in great clumps. "You are what you eat," mother had said, and Lizza now knew what devouring a dead soul really meant.

But Lizza didn't care. If consuming the life essence of a dead soul meant a living death and consuming the essence of a live soul meant new life, Lizza would simply hunt until she found a beautiful soul. Just as mother had healed from her burns, Lizza felt if she consumed the life essence of a beautiful soul she would surely heal. You are what you eat, and Lizza could be beautiful again practically overnight. All she had to do was look for a woman who was beautiful both inside and out. It would be so easy.

Except Lizza discovered she had no control over her wretched body. Instead of searching for a beautiful soul to devour its life essence, Lizza found herself leaving the park in search of more victims. After all, reasoned something else inside of her, now that she knew killing was so easy and so much fun, why shouldn't she use her new-found power to take revenge?

Like Lizza, the woman Lizza had consumed had felt invisible most of her life. She had been ignored by unloving and uncaring parents, bullied by siblings, and forced to marry a man he didn't love. She had no talents and no skills and she hadn't been able to get a job that paid more than the minimum wage after her parents kicked her out of their house the same day she turned eighteen. So she tricked a man, not unlike the way her mother had tricked her father, into marrying her because she was pregnant. And she, also not unlike her mother, had allowed the man she married to beat her and make her feel even more worthless than she already felt. It was one way, perhaps the only way, to keep a roof over her head and food on the table. Perhaps, if she hadn't had children, she might have escaped by slitting her wrists with a razor blade. It wasn't that she loved her children and wanted to stay around to provide for them and to protect them. It was that she hated her husband so much, she wanted to stay around to make life as miserable for him and his two children as he had made life for her. She knew if she died, her husband would rejoice. He'd find another woman—someone younger and prettier—to fill her place. So she stuck around to nag him and yell at the kids and take the beatings she deserved because it was the closest thing to love she knew.

But now all that had changed. She was so driven by anger and hatred that she intended to kill anyone in her way. The woman's dominant adult personality, submerged for an entire lifetime, shoved seven-year-old Lizza aside. Lizza could still see, hear, and feel. But Lizza herself could control nothing.

Bert, the woman's husband, arrived home from work every day at 6:30, half-drunk from happy hour with factory co-workers at a favorite bar. Now the woman hurried to arrive home before her husband did. She wanted to be waiting, invisible, when Bert walked in the door and demanded supper.

She planned to follow Bert around the house as he looked for her and the children in the empty living room, the empty bedrooms, the empty bathroom, and even the empty basement. He would curse her aloud and threaten to beat her bloody unless she came out from wherever she and the children were hiding. Bert knew she was too mousy to leave him, too timid to not be home with supper waiting when he strode through that front door like a king returned to his own kingdom and castle after fighting in some far-away Crusade. She wanted to see the look on Bert's face when he discovered the children were truly gone and the stovetop was empty and cold and his wife was nowhere to be seen.

And then she would swing the big butcher knife she kept in the drawer to the left of the stove straight at his crotch, and she would cut off his manhood and make him eat it instead of the supper he expected. She was the invisible woman, and both she and the knife would remain invisible until she finished cutting.

Once she was sure her husband was dead, she would visit her parents and her older brothers. She would treat her father and brothers the same way she had treated her husband, and then she would think up something special for her mother. Never once, in all the years she had lived with her parents, had her mother even tried to defend her against father and brothers. She could never forgive her mother for that.

Lizza knew of no way to stop the woman from killing her entire family. The woman had already killed both children, and the husband was next.

What didn't make sense to seven-year-old Lizza, at least at first, was the woman's burning hate for her own mother. The woman, whose name Lizza now knew to be Dorothy, hated her mother, whose name was Miranda, more than she hated any of the men.

And then it became clear: what Dorothy hated about her mother was what she hated about herself. Dorothy had become the spitting image of her mother. That was why Dorothy could no longer stand to look at herself in the mirror even long enough to comb her hair.

Lizza, too, looked and acted a lot like her own mother. But mother was beautiful and mother had always protected Lizza from harm. Lizza's mother was nothing like the horrible human mother Dorothy hated. Lizza longed to see her own mother again, to feel protected. If mother were here, she would know what to do. Mother always knew exactly what to do.

But mother wasn't here, and Lizza felt helpless and alone and abandoned, exactly as Dorothy had felt as a child. Dorothy's father had beaten her, her older brothers had sexually abused her, and Dorothy's mother watched and did nothing. Dorothy hated her mother worse than she hated her father, her brothers, and even her husband.

Dorothy's madness was contagious, and Lizza began to hate her own mother, too. Mother had left her all alone in the park to fend for herself, and Lizza made a horrible mistake she never would have been allowed to make if mother had been present. But mother had abandoned Lizza to attend to her own needs. Didn't mother realize Lizza was too young to hunt by herself?

Lizza wanted to punish mother for leaving, and Lizza imagined mother returning to the park much later than planned, searching desperately for the beautiful doll that was no longer there. Mother would worry that she had so badly misjudged her timing that Lizza had shriveled up and faded away while she was gone. It served mother right if mother worried herself to death.

But Lizza knew worry wouldn't kill a witch. Only fire could kill a witch. That was a given. Mother would simply craft a new doll and forget about Lizza entirely.

Lizza couldn't bear the thought of mother making another doll to replace Lizza. After Lizza helped Dorothy, Lizza would beg Dorothy to return the favor and help Lizza kill mother. They could burn down the entire apartment building where mother slept tonight while mother was sound asleep because the only way to kill a witch or a witch's doll was starvation or with fire. If mother had fed today, then mother would need to die by fire.

Mother deserved to die.

"What on earth is wrong with you?" one part of Lizza's mind questioned. "You're only seven. There is so much more mother needs to teach you before you're ready to survive on your own."

"Dorothy will teach me," said the new part of her. "Dorothy is a grown-up. She can be my new mother. I can learn all I need to know from watching her."

"No, you can't," Lizza argued with herself. "You saw what kind of mother Dorothy is. She killed her own children. Do you think she will take better care of you?"

"I can take care of myself."

"No, you can't. Look what happened when you chose Dorothy as a donor. You're falling apart, Lizza. You're rotting from the inside out."

"I can fix that. All I need do to repair the damage is to find a beautiful donor."

"Do you think any donor will let you get close enough to capture her essence? The way you look now, you'd scare away any woman who possessed enough sense to make a difference in the way you look and feel. You can never be well again without mother's help."

"I can too!"

"Can not!"

Lizza arrived at Dorothy's house at 6:10. She had more than enough time to go into the kitchen and find the butcher knife she wanted in the drawer next to the stove. The knife had a nine-inch-long razor-sharp stainless steel blade Dorothy used to carve pork roasts and Thanksgiving turkeys. Now she intended to use the knife to carve up her husband.

Lizza didn't want to watch, but she couldn't close her eyes and she couldn't turn away. What little was left of the beautiful Lizza felt powerless against the dominating influence of corruption that infused every cell of her body.

The doorknob turned, the door swung open on squeaking hinges, and a big man wearing dirty oil-stained khaki-colored work clothes swaggered into the room, tossed his empty lunch pail onto the kitchen table, looked around for his family who obviously weren't in the kitchen, and shouted, "Where the fuck is everyone?" as he balled up his fists and angrily strode into the living room.

Dorothy made Lizza follow the man through the entire house before she stabbed him in the back. Then Dorothy rolled his bleeding body over, opened his pants, and sliced off his private parts.

She forced the bloody flesh between his slack jaws.

Then Dorothy left her own house and walked to her parents' house. When she finished with her parents, she paid a visit to each of her brothers.

What little was left of the old Lizza heard the new Lizza direct Dorothy to find a book of matches and bottles of flammable fluids. The new Lizza guided Dorothy to the apartment where mother slept.

"You can't do this," whispered what was left of the old Lizza.

"Just watch me," said the new Lizza.

The old Lizza could do nothing as Dorothy and the new Lizza spread accelerant around the building where mother slept. The old Lizza tried desperately to keep the new Lizza from striking a match. For a brief moment, Lizza called upon the last of her old energy to mentally arm wrestle the new Lizza to a stand-still. The match moved an inch toward the striker pad on the matchbook, moved slowly away an inch, gradually moved back again. Back and forth it went, an inch at a time.

But the effort eventually proved futile, and the old Lizza's energy was nearly extinct when the match ignited, dropped onto the accelerant, and the building Lizza and mother had called home for nearly three months suddenly burst into flames.

Lizza watched, horrified, as residents evacuated the building. Some exited screaming, their clothes and hair ablaze, their skin blistering and turning black. Some made it out unscathed. Mother didn't come out at all, nor did the woman whose apartment they had shared.

Lizza, what was left of the old Lizza, cried inwardly. She couldn't remember crying since she was a baby, and today—in one single day—she had cried twice. When she cried earlier in the park, it was only because she was afraid for herself and she didn't want to die. Now she cried because mother was dead and all beauty in the world seemed gone forever. She wept not for herself. She cried for mother, and she cried for the others who needlessly lost their lives in the fire.

Dorothy and the new Lizza laughed as they watched the building burn.

Behind them, from the buildings and sidewalks across the street, people rushed to extinguish burning clothes on burn victims and to render first aid. Lizza could hear sirens in the distance. Fire trucks were on their way, but they would arrive too late to save mother and other occupants still inside.

While Dorothy and the other Lizza were laughing and had their attention focused on the flames, Lizza was able to turn herself visible. The new Lizza sensed the change, and she took her eyes off the burning building long enough to instinctively look around to see if any of the bystanders posed any kind of threat. When her eyes made contact with the eyes of a young woman in a nurse's uniform coming rapidly toward her to ask if she needed assistance, the old Lizza reached out with the last of her fading strength and extracted the healing life-essence of the nurse before the new Lizza could prevent it. As love and caring and concern flooded Lizza's body with new vitality, Lizza felt Dorothy and the other Lizza wither away like fruit left too long on the vine.

Lizza was back in control of her body again, and she instantly dashed toward the burning building to try to rescue mother. Though she knew in her heart it was already too late, she had to try. So what if she burned up herself? She didn't care about herself anymore. All she cared about was mother.

But before she could enter the building, the roof collapsed and falling debris and flying sparks drove everyone back. Lizza felt adult hands grab onto her arms and carry her to safety. In her hurry to save mother, she suddenly realized, she had neglected to render herself invisible. Someone had thought they were saving an ordinary seven-year-old girl—not a living doll—from the flames.

This time Lizza had chosen wisely and well. The donor, a rather ordinary-looking woman in her mid-twenties, possessed such inner beauty that she had healed Lizza almost immediately. Lizza's hair was again long and silky and blonde, her skin flawless, her eyes bright blue like the sky on a cloudless day.

"Are you all right, little girl?" asked the man who had rescued her. "Where's your mother? Or your father? Aren't they with you?"

When the man mentioned mother, Lizza's eyes once again flooded with tears. Lizza had no father, but she had once had a mother who had nourished her and cared for her and carefully trained her.

And, though neither witches nor dolls had a soul, Lizza knew that mother had loved her as much, if not more, than most mothers who did have souls.

And Lizza, who had been too young before to know what love was, now knew that mother had loved her and Lizza had loved her mother even more than Lizza had loved herself. Lizza knew what love was because she had learned first what hate was and had rejected it.

Fire trucks arrived on the scene, and everyone was pushed back out of the way. As soon as the man let go of Lizza's arm, she turned herself invisible and slipped away from the crowd.

Mother was gone, and Lizza was all alone in the world. Lizza had no idea if there were other witches left alive anywhere in the entire world, or any witches' dolls. Was she the only living doll? Or were there others like her somewhere?

Lizza was young, perhaps too young to survive on her own. But she would try. Mother had taught her well. Lizza had a fighting chance.

Lizza decided it was time to leave this city of so many memories, both good and bad. Mother said they would need to leave soon anyway, and Lizza knew how to hop a bus or a train and go anywhere she wanted. Lizza had never been on an airplane before, but she didn't suppose getting onto an airplane would be much different than getting on a bus. She might even travel to distant lands in search of others of her kind. Perhaps, someday in the not so distant future, she would find another doll or another witch who would show her how to make a doll of her own.

Lizza wondered what kind of a mother a doll would make.

Lizza was unaware of the beautiful young-looking woman, hidden in the crowd across the street, who watched Lizza's every move even when Lizza turned invisible to ordinary human eyes. Perhaps it was smoke from the burning building that brought tears into the beautiful young woman's blue eyes, or perhaps it was recalling the painful lesson her own mother had taught her when she had been only seven and newly weaned. Two soul-feeders in the same town at the same time was one too many, and the human herd would soon notice so many disappearances and the witch hunts of old would begin all over again. How many witches and witch's dolls had to be burned at the stake before it became obvious what needed to be done?

"Faire thee well, child," mother whispered as she wiped tears from her eyes. Severing the umbilical was painful but necessary. "Faire thee well, darling Lizza."

Soon it would be time to craft a new doll. Mother tried to cheer herself up by thinking of names for her next baby.

▲

Gut Punch

by Jason A. Wyckoff

"Antiphon! Antiphon! It sloughs history!"

Her laugh is fay. She wobbles the royal wave; one imagines wine sloshing from a goblet. In any other setting, I *would* think she was drunk or high; I've certainly seen her that way often enough. But I'm told she has been under observation for five days now. My mother is in a robin's egg gown, sitting on a cot in a locked room, talking to no one.

I can't watch her anymore. I never loved her, but this hurts—it hurts me (*sans* pathos) because however pitiful the circumstance, however strange the performance, the comportment is too familiar, re-opening every wound of my youth.

Dr. Duenger leads me back to his office and bids me sit. He dawdles as though composing his thoughts; it's a performance to add weight.

I don't have the patience. "What did she take?" I ask. "What could do that—cause permanent damage?"

"Well, that's just the thing, Mr. Wince." He milks the pause to recoup the drama I deprived him of. "The toxicology report came back...negative."

I chuckle. "That's impossible."

Spock cocks an eyebrow. "Ah, yes. Her history."

"Ah, yes, her history," I echo.

"You didn't know, then?"

He has me on something; it annoys me and clearly delights him. "Know what?"

"Your mother has been going to meetings since last February. She's been clean for more than a year."

That's unexpected, but I'm not invested enough to be impressed. "A backslide, then. No, wait." I hold up a hand. "I know—the toxicology report came back negative."

He shrugs. "We were hoping you could shed some light...but you say you've had no contact with her?"

Out of the blue, she'd called twice in the last month. I hadn't answered. "No contact," I say. "Not for a while now."

"A shame." He sighs almost wistfully.

"A necessity. How did she end up here?"

"Her sponsor hadn't heard from her in a week. He went to check on her. He called us right away."

"She was…like that?" I nod towards the hallway.

"She appears to be in a state of arrested euphoria, as it were."

No bad deed goes unrewarded, it seems. "That's your diagnosis?"

"No, no. That's an observation. The problem with her diagnosis is… well, you could throw a dart and hit one that fit, as long as you include the caveat that should disqualify it."

Ah, so *that's* how it's done.

He goes on, "The euphoria is somewhat symptomatic of the manic period of bi-polar disorder, though she shows no signs of agitation, and is, in fact, quite compliant."

He smiles as though he's just congratulated a parent on their child no longer eating paste.

"Also, actual psychosis is rare with bi-polar disorder; her level of extreme dissociation is more indicative of schizophrenia, but that condition is often linked with an *inability* to feel joy. And while she is not withdrawn *per se,* she is non-communicative in such a way that we cannot establish any sort of self-valuation, which would be instructive. In the past, we might have identified 'schizoaffective disorder', a sort of broad-based diagnosis which has recently fallen out of favor, but might actually be germane in this instance."

He leans forward, interlaces his fingers, and props his chin on his thumbs. He stares at the wall behind me, as though having judged me an inadequate audience.

"The problem is exacerbated when one considers that all of those conditions are developmental, with initial symptoms generally manifesting during early adulthood. It is unlikely one of these disorders would suddenly bloom at this stage of life absent a secondary factor, possibly physiological in nature. Nevertheless, as the administration of anti-psychotics is appropriate for all the aforementioned diagnoses, we pursued that course. But she has remained unresponsive. Typically, we would expect *some* sort of behavioral response."

"You mean you gave her drugs that should have knock her senseless, but didn't."

His expression is smug in its flatness. "I would hardly put it like that. But, yes, her condition has remained resistant…one might almost say, 'obdurate'. For example, she hasn't slept since she's been here."

I scowl, wondering what kind of quack factory Mommy Dearest has landed in. "You haven't sedated her?"

"In general, we avoid sedating patients with a history of substance abuse," Duenger drips, as though I should know better. "We strive to restore balance by putting our patients on their own two feet, not by giving them crutches. Nevertheless, in extraordinary cases like your mother's, we will prescribe drugs called hypnotics, or soporifics. These have had no effect. Concerned for her well-being, and against my own better judgment, I even approved Seconal. This, too, proved unhelpful. Some impulse spurred me to run another tox screen, and *those* results were most curious of all, as there again appeared to be no trace of drugs in her blood—even *after* she'd been given a barbiturate! Now, I can't account for that, but it did bring to mind another unlikely possibility. Tell me, when your mother was sober, did she ever have seizures, or was she…eh, fearful?"

I wasn't expecting a question about her *not* drinking, but the answer is easy enough. "No, she always felt good about it. Until she felt so good about being so damn good and responsible that she'd reward herself the only way she knew how."

Duenger tapped a pen on his desk pad. "Yes, well, it was a bit of a longshot. There's a neurological phenomenon called 'kindling' wherein the harmful effects of withdrawal become increasingly more severe from instance to instance; one possible outcome is the development of psychosis in the substance abuser."

"Wait—you're saying that *sobriety* drove my mother insane?"

He waves it away. "Again—it is unlikely, especially without precedent, which you say she has not demonstrated."

I have no reason to feel ashamed of how long I've been away, and of being ignorant of the possibility of my mother's behavior changing, but for some reason I don't want to share that with the good doctor. He shrugs as though already aware of what I don't choose to acknowledge. Naturally, I find it irksome.

I say, "You mentioned a 'secondary factor'."

"Yes. Of course we tested for several neurological diseases, electrolyte imbalances and mineral deficiencies and such, but we saw nothing unusual in her blood panels beyond an elevated white cell count—nothing particularly alarming, given her condition. She had several bed sores that needed tending."

"She was bedridden? I thought you said she wasn't lethargic."

"Not under our observation." Duenger is almost glowing with suppressed joy. Who doesn't love a good mystery, right? I bet if I search his hard drive, I'll find the précis of a medical journal submission.

"You mentioned testing for neurological disease—so I can assume you've run an MRI?" I grumble.

"Yesterday: nothing." He pauses again, almost daring me to raise another challenge. When I don't, he says, "So we return to the original question: How could she be demonstrating what has all the hallmarks of a drug-induced psychosis despite ostensibly being clean and without anything showing up in our tests? I've begun to wonder if perhaps she's been affected by a contaminant of some sort, not something we would call a drug in the classic sense."

I have no idea what that means, but I don't bite on it.

He continues, "I suspect an environmental factor. I'd like to go with you to your mother's house for a look around, if you don't mind."

Light bulb. "That's why you called me."

"Well, it was time," he says, and lets it drift between meanings—time for him to call the reluctant emergency contact, time at last for me to come home.

I'm just plain mad at this point. I jump up and head for the door. "Take me back there. Let's try this again. I want to go in."

There's one last bit of theatre at the door to her cell. The orderly pauses, key at the lock. He's a black guy whose size alone would've gotten him an athletic scholarship to warm the pine as a defensive lineman. He looks at Dr. Duenger, who looks at me. "Open it, goddammit," I command.

We three enter. My mother says, "These clotted mountains are naught but waterfalls a-borning!" The laugh follows. Everything gets a laugh, I'm guessing.

I step forward and crouch in her line of sight. "Hey, it's me. It's Devin. It's your son." That doesn't get a laugh. That gets nothing. "Mom," and the word is strange, "Mom, it's your son."

She doesn't see me. She's watching a channel I can't subscribe to. "Delight cannot be obtained by craving. For unjust rains fall upon even the most skilled of swallowers."

I don't see the point in trying any further. "Forget it," I say, mostly to myself. I turn to go out. I'm in no mood to pick through her word salad for kernels of truth. She can catch her own bus back.

"Devin," she says, and I freeze.

I turn back. *Now* she sees me and it is infinitely worse than when I wasn't there. Her eyes are singing, screaming; they're loud eyes and the message they send is overwhelming. I can't look at her. Her voice, the one saying all that crazy, faux-literary shit, that was her voice. But her talking to *me*, it's wrong somehow; there's an unrecognizable tone—caring? I don't know whose voice it is that says, "Devin, let's all be rotting children again."

And I'm *gone.*

* * * *

Doctor Duenger is eager to get into my mother's house—my childhood home—right away. He pouts when I tell him I'll call him in the morning to say when we can meet there. I was seven hours on the road straight to the laughing academy, and those few moments with mom sucked out whatever life I had left in me. For that reason, I opt for a motel. I could go 'home'—I really don't believe the doc's whole 'environmental factor' thesis—but I don't want to cross that threshold when I'm already beat down. Emotions? No, thank you. Gimme suspicious stains and AC you can't turn down.

This isn't the town I remember. Some store fronts have changed, and those that haven't are shabbier and seem smaller. I feel alienated from these streets in a way I couldn't be if they were merely unfamiliar. Of course, I'm the only one gawking. Even in a small town, natives are accorded the right to be blasé about incremental change.

I'm on edge, expecting a meeting, but I don't see anyone I know. I have near-meaningless interaction with the motel clerk and the quick-stop cashier and that's it. I feel my homecoming should be more portentous. But, perhaps because I have no inkling what sort of omen I might expect or what it could possibly signify, I am left unsatisfied. I can't divine the feeling I'm supposed to have, and my hometown doesn't care for me any more than it ever did. I feel like an excised mole someone is trying to push back on their skin. Deprived of definable gravitas, I wallow in void for half an hour before I finally do something smart and call Joseph.

Joseph handles me with ease. He coaxes a few monosyllabic grunts from me as a courtesy, and then masterfully monopolizes the conversation. He takes me through our neighborhood with the minutiae of his day; he leads me to our apartment with a question about sconces that requires no answer; he summons the corgis and kissy-faces with them into the receiver. And he knows exactly when to press forward.

"Did you go to the house?"

"No," I say, "I put it off until tomorrow."

"I think that's smart. You've had enough to deal with for one day."

"That's how I saw it. I don't know if I even want to go there at all."

"Then don't," he says.

"No. I have to." I quote the doctor, "'It's time'." I almost feel guilty fishing for confidence in Joseph's pond.

"When you're ready," Joseph says with a tone that tells me whatever decision I make will be the right one in his eyes. "Call me while you're there, if you like."

"Thanks, but I probably won't. The doctor will be with me. Not content to poke around skulls, he's taken to houses. This is a man for whom no cigar is just a cigar."

Joseph teases me, "You know what I love about you? So many angry teen queens grow up to be well-adjusted gays, but you—you have really stayed the course."

"To thine own self and all that shit," I reply.

Like an idiot, I look around me and take in the anonymity of my surroundings. I squirm as that oppressive 'limbo' sensation thickens the air between stucco and low-pile. "I haven't seen anybody I know," I say.

"Well, it's not like you can go back to your high school to find your old pals." This is a joke; he knows high school was miserable.

"It's true, there's no one I *want* to see. But...the doctor says she's been clean for more than a year. I guess I need confirmation... Maybe I want to hear what she's like when she's been clean for that long."

"It's got nothing to do with you unless you want it to." He pauses. "Didn't you use to go to church? You could try there."

"Jesus! Tomorrow's Sunday."

"Yes, Jesus, tomorrow is Sunday. Maybe your mother kept going."

"Maybe she started going," I correct him. "I mean, we went, but only intermittently. We probably would've been strictly C and E crowd if it wasn't for her chasing absolution every time she flipped over the same old leaf. And me in tow." I sigh. "I mean, I guess it's as good a place as any..."

"I knew it!" Joseph exclaims. "I knew you still had some of that old time religion in you."

I hate to think that might be true. "The only temple I worship is your body; yours, the only altar I kneel before."

I actually startle him to silence for a few seconds. Then he says, "Devin, darling, I can't tell if you're being sweet or being a total wanker."

I lay back on the bed. "Can't a man be both?"

I hear his cheek rub against the phone as he smiles. "Do you need me to tuck you in?"

* * * *

The gauntlet of the narthex: Uncertain smiles under flickers of almost-recognition or awkward flashes of actual recognition. Why did I come here? I can't be the only one questioning my presence. It's not His house, it's theirs.

Relax, I tell myself. It's a moderate church, and you have a history here, such as it may be. No one is going to chase you out with a pitchfork. Be charitable, or at least join the charade. As always—endure.

Besides, it can't be said that you don't clean up nice. Part of the *other* heritage.

I sit through the service. The pastor is new to me. I could sketch him entirely with circles. He is genially red-faced in front of his languid congregation. I recall the prayers and hymns with ease, but I can't invest in them. They are like reruns stripped of the canned laughter which ironically made them seem real, left as incomplete archival footage from that grand old show that once fooled me into believing I really was a part of a live studio audience that stretched over the world and persevered through the centuries.

The homily instructs us to guard against pessimism.

I review as many stained glass windows as I can look at without obviously ignoring the sermon. I still see some magic in the colored glass (depicting bible stories and apostles—not *saints;* we don't do saints). I am momentarily entranced by Abraham and Isaac. Post intercession, of course—haloed Abraham holds his son in one arm and stretches a grateful hand towards heaven. There is something comforting in the simple forced perspective—in the very idea of a verdant slope directly behind, awaiting their descent. A hill which I see now has one small, discolored blot, of what can only be described as *stained* stained glass, grey humus to the green grass. And I am nearly sick when I notice baby Isaac looks not to heaven or to his father, but back at the altar.

Afterwards, a few people, given time to confirm that I am who they think I am, approach to say hello, to ask how I've been, what I've been up to, *where* I've been. As surprised to see me as they are, they are confused why my mother isn't with me. It's confirmed for me she's become a regular. A few people have heard she's been 'sick', but no more than that, and I don't elucidate. I tell them, "She's resting". I can see in their eyes they're wondering if she's plunged off the wagon; I'm surprised that the concern seems genuine (as opposed to, "Please let us know if we need to duck and cover"). I tell them I guess she might be back next week, and they seem relieved.

Mrs. Mason has conducted the youth choir since long before I mangled a tune. She says, "You're such a good boy to help your mother. Tell Bea I'll pray for her."

I say, "Thank you," and not, *You'd better pray for a miracle, Mrs. Mason, because if you saw what I saw, you'd know there's no fucking way she's coming back next week—or maybe ever.* "It's been a long time since I've been home. I guess…mom's been doing well?"

"Oh, yes, she's become a valued member of the congregation." She pats me on my shoulder and smiles. "You should be proud."

The encouragement means either she knows I'm not, or she doesn't know enough and thinks I could be.

"Was she here last week?" I ask.

She cocks her head and considers the ceiling. "No, no, I don't remember her being here. But she hasn't lingered to chat the last few times I've seen her. She seemed anxious to be home. Honestly…well, maybe I shouldn't say. But, I thought she might have a boyfriend. Which, really…it's time, don't you think?"

"Her happiness is all that matters," I say, not, *if you had any idea what manner of man she used to call 'boyfriend', you wouldn't wish that for her,* or, *can't we all stop saying, 'it's time'?*

"So, how does it feel to be back home?" Mrs. Mason asks.

"I guess it's time I found out," I say, corralling the frown that accompanies the thought, *no, I guess we can't.* "I stayed at the Comfort Palace last night. I…wasn't ready." I feel exposed; I don't know why I confided that.

To my surprise, Mrs. Mason isn't nonplussed, but responds equally frankly. "Your mother broke through," she says, "sometime last year. Cast off her shackles, as it were. She never told me what it was that finally changed in her or in her life."

I remembered how I quit smoking. "In my experience, the only real motivator for personal change is disgust."

She smiles softly and chides me, "Perhaps that is what it takes to *get* to that moment of decision. But one hopes she turned to God in that moment, and it was He who lifted her up and transformed her. I can tell you this: She did mention to me once… You shouldn't feel guilty."

"I don't." Ah, at least *that* automatic defense has not been compromised.

"Of course. Good." She nods, and then touches my arm again. "She said that one of the things that…held her back for so long was how she, she blamed herself…for you. For how she raised you!" she adds hurriedly. "For how she didn't *care* for you correctly." She sighs exasperatedly and removes her glasses to polish them on a silk scarf. "I'm sorry; I'm not saying this right."

"No, I understand," I assure her. "Recrimination is a cycle. I know it well."

So mother cast off her guilt? Well, hallelujah and pass me a virgin daiquiri. How *neat* for her. How positively *white.*

I excuse myself, after promising Mrs. Mason once more that I understand perfectly what she meant. I definitely do not want her to stammer through explaining she didn't mean to say mother blamed herself for my sexuality. I think we're both uncomfortable enough already.

On my way to my car I call Duenger to tell him to meet me at the house in an hour if he still wants in.

Oh, yes, oh, yes.

I stop at a chain family joint and pick a spot at the 'bar'. The smell of warm maple-flavored corn syrup suffuses the air. Who am I to deny its flirtation? French toast and coffee. There is lipstick on my coffee cup and I wonder glumly if it's meant to be a comment or just the random spoil of inattentiveness. There's no telling; the waitress would call her executioner 'Honey'.

"Whenever you're ready," she says when she slips me the bill.

* * * *

Unlike every other structure in town, the house does not look smaller. Two stories and a cellar, side and back yards. It was always more than we two needed; it had been meant for a family, after all. I had a younger brother, Chuck. The inevitable divorce split my family in the middle. It was as though my parents went to Solomon and took him at his word. Either my dad thought two kids would be too hard on him, or maybe just too hard to win, because of course my mother fought him for custody out of spite. Maybe dad misinterpreted the mutual contempt my mother and I shared for closeness; I remember him as fairly clueless. Either way, I'm sure it was easier to 'cut bait' on the longer line. He and Chuck called twice during the year after they left. They died together seven years later with the rest of his new family from carbon monoxide poisoning. Sleep tight. Mother flared for a month; I couldn't have left her for the funerals even if I'd wanted to.

I pull into the driveway behind an unmarked white van with diagonal grating spanning its back windows. I find them on the porch. Duenger paces anxiously. The lummox orderly, smoking a cigarette, shares the creaking porch swing with the shifting limpness that is my mother, who is dressed but otherwise the same as I'd left her. I assume she just said something hilarious. She doesn't see me.

"What the hell is she doing here?" I yell.

"Ah! Mr. Wince. Let's get right to it, shall we?"

"Did you hear me?" I challenge.

Duenger furrows his brow, confused—no, he didn't hear me. Then it processes. "Oh, yes—I thought it best to bring your mother to the origination point of her…" he twirls a hand. It strikes me odd that a psychiatrist can't conjure a euphemism for 'mental collapse'. *'Episode', for God's sake.* "I thought it would be enlightening to see if anything set her off."

Still hot, I say, "I don't see how that would be therapeutic. Besides, you said you suspected an environmental factor."

"Indeed, I did," he says, "and 'environment' is what we call our physical and psychical surroundings."

I've never heard *that* definition before.

He goes on, "So the...contaminant might be chemical or biological, or even allegorical. Just as memory is tied to scent, or a sad picture makes us sad. You see?"

"No," I answer. I most certainly do not.

"If we went inside, perhaps everything will reveal itself," Duenger encourages.

Perhaps because I'm not getting the explanation I want from the doctor, I look at the orderly. He shrugs disinterestedly. That should be all I expect, but I stare at him anyway. He chuckles and flicks the spent butt into a barberry bush. "If you want my professional opinion *as an orderly,*" he says, "I think your moms is batshit loco." He stands and pulls my mother to her feet effortlessly. He mocks me, "I *do* hope this helps you on your path to understanding and acceptance."

The doc frets, "I really don't see what the problem is."

I frown, spin and lurch for the handle. "It's unlocked," I announce. I regard the doctor suspiciously. "You could've gone right in without me."

"Legally, I couldn't enter," he assures me, as though the law prohibitively affects physics. "Besides, we need to go in there as a *unit.*"

I don't understand the distinction. I'm too annoyed to care.

"Hey, I'm hourly," laughs the orderly. "Long as I'm done by five, you can do what the hell you want."

Why *am* I fighting the inevitable? I open the door. I regret it.

"Damn!" the orderly recoils with his free arm to his nose. "And I hose down folks that shit themselves!"

The scent is noxious, but it's not shit. And the fumes don't burn my soft palate like so many chemical smells do. It's not sweet like rot, either, or reeking like fish, or rotten like phosphorous. I can't classify it. It's aggressively damp, somehow, and fetid, like the burning fur of a sick dog was dowsed with vinegar.

Duenger marches past me into the house. "Let's see inside, then. Come on, everyone in!" He sees our dubious faces and scrunched noses. "It's not so bad inside," he assures us, "after the initial shock is processed. You'll see." But even mother has changed her tune—unpleasantly. She is groaning.

"You don't think *that* is what drove her nuts?" I demand.

He says coolly, "It couldn't have been. You'll remember, nothing was mentioned about any smell when her sponsor discovered her, or when the EMTs arrived to assist. Something must have spoiled, that's all."

The reasoning is sound, but I don't like it.

The orderly swings my mother over the threshold. "Let's get this the hell over with," he barks.

I follow him in. I hit the switch just inside the door; the bulb overhead only slightly un-dims the interior from the grey day. My breath catches. The dimensions are so familiar, the floor plan set in my memory, but everything else is different. Why wouldn't it be? I haven't been in this house for a decade. The walls are a different color, the furniture is new, the giant tube TV and its pedestal are absent; the flat screen on the wall seems out of place. But the real difference is the condition of things—clean. No, not *clean,* in the standard housekeeping sense, as it is obvious that any concerns about cleanliness vacated with mom's wits, but at least kept up, modern-ish—the decrepitude on display appears recent and not resulting from year-on-year neglectful attrition, the décor of the burnout I remember from my youth. This is my impression of one room—the glazed sliding doors that lead to the dining room are closed.

So enraptured am I by trivialities no one else could care about that it is the orderly's exertions that finally draw my attention, not my mother's violent shaking.

"Come on, now!" he says, his massive arms around her.

She twists, struggling to get free. "No!" she screams. "No! It's bad. I threw up in the tub and it got everywhere!"

"Jesus! Get her out of here!" I instruct the orderly.

"No!" countermands Duenger. "Let her go. Release her!"

"What? She'll bolt!" I yell.

"You must do as I say. Do it! Let her go!"

The orderly doesn't release her so much as he just drops his arms slack. Even his head dips sideways and his mouth opens. His eyelids flit rapidly. I wonder if *he* is having an attack. Mother, however, free from his grasp and contrary to my expectation, sighs and rocks forward and back, as though once more in the throes of her gentle euphoria. A shudder runs through the orderly as though waking from a nap. He looks embarrassed at first, and then he smiles like a child.

Only then do I notice that Duenger has slid wide the glazed doors.

The smell is worse, ten times worse, but its foul bloom is so effervescent in my sinuses that it feels like gas fills my head and lifts me and I wonder if I am standing or floating.

The dining room writhes. Some sort of opaque, gelatinous substance foams over every surface. The layer is thin farthest from the staircase, such that the hard angles of a cupboard are discernible to my left, and I can even see portions of the wooden frame around the door to the kitchen. But towards the staircase the mass grows halfway to the ceiling. It piles upon itself to form clumsily wavering stalagmites, a giant anemone prodding mindlessly at the air, its tentacles failing, slopping and consumed again in the roiling lower body, the hopeless toil repeating. It is white and green and brown and blue and every color, but none pure, all soiled, a retch of pointillism.

I threw up in the tub and it got everywhere.

The floor quavers as the orderly suddenly drops to his knees, his arms at his sides, palms open to the front. Tears stream down his cheeks as he laughs like a cold engine trying to start, "Huh-huh-huh-huh-huh-huh-huh-huh!"

I wonder what he sees. I look again at the alien mound in the dining room and I discern shapes forming in the stuff. I cannot tell yet what they might become, but they are distinct from the reaching spires.

Yes, that's a face there.

It's gone.

Two rough faces now, twin sides to the same head, as Janus—my father and brother? They separate, become a woman's breasts. One raises, arcs and looms over the other one, which flattens, to form something like the lopsided oval trough in a wave, and then both sides resolve into an image of much greater complexity. Adam reclines and stretches lazily while God reaches towards him from the clouds. And Adam has my face. But in place of Michelangelo's limp sprout a segmented erection grows dollop by dollop, and as the creator melts back to formlessness, his arm droops such that he looks as though he reaches for it.

Then everything ripples from the middle; a bubble emerges and then flattens forward. The images shift to fine focus as every pustule in the gangrenous mass becomes a precise tile in a mottled mosaic, a blot of ink on a filthy Bayeux Tapestry. Scenes blend, melt and congeal: My brother falling from the cigar tree, too disgusted by the ants filing up between his small hands to hold on; the looming mustachioed face of a disposable stud pushing a reefer on me, holding back the laughter my mother in the background cannot; flashes of television memories as the South Tower falls and Buffy kisses Spike; my Night of the Pills freshman year in college that I botched so badly that no one even knew until I told Joseph; and finally Joseph in person, volunteered by a bevy of clueless pensioners at the Luau to join the Hula while I laughed until I cried; and the scene swallows itself into the frame of an asylum window behind which my mother waves loosely.

The good doctor is disrobing my mother with clear intent. I'm angry for only a second before the tug of conscience vanishes. I am fascinated by the sudden vacancy. Duenger catches my eye.

"The first horizon has wilted!" he declares. "Mark well to cut the rattle from the baby's hand!" And I read that same desperation in his eyes that I'd seen in my mother's, the hidden aspect in the cloud of disingenuous, salacious joy, that thing that is the *only* thing that should be there: terror.

Anger rouses me. I understand the set-up now and I accuse him: *You've been here before! You're infected, just like my mother, and you brought me here to infect me, too!*

Only what I say is, "Rondeau! A crooked man walks a straight path, a pocketful of tadpoles to the circus!"

I understand the terror now. The nonsense is upon us. We can't communicate. My neck spasms at the base of my skull and snaps my head back. I blink repeatedly. I try again: *You won't make me like you!*

"All's Hell that ends!"

My compromised protestations are ignored. The doctor is rolling my mother over in the slop. He seems almost bewildered about how to penetrate her. I want to run but instead I begin weaving on my feet counterclockwise. The orderly bends forward, smearing a putrid kaleidoscope over the floor, ooh-ing and ah-ing.

What is this stuff—this psychic mold, this cancerous ectoplasm, this froth of decadence? What foul wonder is this that has ruined my mother and compelled the mad doctor to evangelize? I know it. I know it. I know it. It is corpses in our heads. It is the compost of souls. When spirit breaks down, where does it go? It is in all of us; it is ten millennium of rotted thought from whence new ideas spring; it carries in spoiled spores on the waves between us.

Yes. Yes. And occasionally it gets caught in the deeper pits of the emptier husks. It materializes and festers in our guts, germinating in a caul of bile and anxiety, accreting mass as a bezoar, corrupting and killing only to die along with us, unless…unless a person frees herself.

My mother decided to let go of the pain she suffered for her failure. For her benefit alone, she absolved herself and left the mess in the tub. Because I wasn't there to tell her she had no right to take on my suffering in the first place.

So I yell—no words, no meaning, just anger. No one else gives a damn, but I roar. And there is a crumpling inside me and sparks move my limbs. I am outside before I know how I've gotten free.

I don't know what to do. I know I need to get away. Primal thought saved me, primal thought moves me. I want to go to ground. But home is not an option. The church? Services are over—and what should I say? I go to the motel. I have to call Joseph. My strength.

I feel terrible. I can barely fit the key. The room spins and I collapse on the bed. I'm nauseous. Maybe… I feel it's very important to say something reasonable. I have to make my words work. I try…I try with the one clear thought that remains.

"How…how dare she?" I ask.

I am still sick. My insides twist. But my scalp tingles and a feeling of minty lightness brushes my skin. And so I begin to smile, because I know it is so stupid. It is so absolutely stupid.

I chuckle. "Don't you remember that you don't care?"

My stomach roils. Fluid pushes upwards. I scramble for the toilet. I puke violently, repeatedly, french toast and coffee and so, so much more.

I collapse back against the wall of the bathroom. My chest is heaving, my heart fluttering. I am weak but I feel better. As bad as it smells, it takes me a few minutes to gather the reserves to flush the toilet. I lean forward. Perverse curiosity grips me. The experience was so brutal, the purge so cathartic; I *have* to look at what came out of me.

Oh.

Oh, Joseph *must* see this. ▲

Castle Csejthe

Ashley Dioses

In corridors of stone, the claws of girls engrave
The walls with horizontal marks of darkest red.
The blood and broken nails embed and paint, then pave
The way toward the torture chambers, realms of dread.

The pallid ladies, beautiful as ocean's foam,
Were playthings of the Countess, and their prizèd bloo
Flowed forth alike a crimson sea, where she would comb
Her hair with it or bathe beneath its endless flood.

In castle Csejthe, hell awaits those maidens pure
Of heart and pure of mind, for Bathory desires
Them both. She steals their very breath to find a cure
For even death, till life eternal she acquires!

Educational Upgrade
by Bret McCormick

He couldn't believe how dingy the neighborhood was. This was the part of town slackers went to for tattoos and piercings. Maybe a decent mechanic was nestled into one of these side streets. It was possible, but an honest mechanic? More likely a chop shop. For sure you could find drug dealers on every block if you knew how to go about that sort of thing. Murray cruised slowly past the parked cars that crowded the curb, looking for 4315. Most of the buildings seemed to have no address numbers posted. He decided that was no accident. The people who lived here didn't want to be found. He looked at the back of Harrison's business card for the hundredth time, reading the address scribbled there. Yes, he was in the right place; Granada Street. Not Granada Boulevard, that nice thoroughfare running through the south side of town in the new Medical District, as he'd originally assumed. He *had* called ahead to verify. It was definitely on Granada *Street.* If anyone other than Harrison had made the recommendation, Murray would have cut and run when he saw this seedy district in all its pitifully decaying detail. Half the businesses were boarded up, covered with graffiti. Still, he knew for a fact that Harrison earned twice the amount of money he did at Gelco. That was a fact he had verified with Donna in accounting. If Harrison had been through this program and vouched for it, it was legit.

He spotted 4315, an old flat-roofed office building of the style that was popular in the late fifties and early sixties. It was a drab shade of beige. Some paint salesman might have called it *'Desert Sand'* or *'Parchment,'* but to Murray it just looked like bargain-bin paint. Still it was the only building on that block with *fresh* paint and the address clearly marked in large black numerals. With increasing irritation he noted that there were no empty parking spaces anywhere near his destination. He'd have to scout a spot and walk. Hopefully, his car would still be there, unmolested when he returned. The nearest curbside opening large enough for him to parallel park was two blocks away. He was not encouraged when a group of idle young men, hanging out on a stairway, took note of the loud beeping of his car's locking mechanism.

"What the fuck," he muttered, looking over his shoulder and hoping for the best, "Harrison, this better be worth it." Reluctantly, he turned left at the corner, taking note of the street sign. The side street was Vista. He could remember that.

The door to 4315 was painted a bright blue. That seemed an odd choice to Murray. He opened the door and walked into an empty reception area. A sign designed to look like a clock said "back at 1:30." His wristwatch indicated it was 12:05. Surely someone was expecting him. He'd made an appointment for God's sake!

"Hello," he called, starting down the narrow hallway that led away from the reception area into the belly of the building. There was no reply. He passed a couple of doors marked "Men" and "Ladies", then checked behind a third door to find it was a supply closet, a poorly stocked supply closet. He was encouraged by a metallic rattle coming from the vicinity of a fourth door. Murray entered the room to find a slight man with his back to the door, watering plants in pots on the window sill. "Hello," he said again.

The guy turned around, his dark, intense eyes peering out from under a tangle of wooly, shoulder-length hair. "Oh, hey man. You Murray?" The man smiled and set his watering can down on the top of a filing cabinet. He rubbed his hand on his pant leg before stretching it across the desk and offering it to Murray. Without a word, Murray shook the man's hand, all the while thinking he'd seen the guy before. "Have a seat," the man said, sweeping the tangle of hair out of his face and dropping into the battered chair behind the desk.

Murray sat and glanced at the card in his hand for the hundred and first time. "Are you Daniel?" He asked, reading the man's name as Harrison had scribbled it two days before.

"That's me! Great to meet you. Harrison told us you'd be coming in." The guy's grin was almost intimidating. Murray stared at him, still trying to figure out why the man's face was so familiar, then all at once it came to him.

"You look like that guy," he said, wagging a finger across the desk at Daniel. "The cult thing in Hollywood..."

"Charlie? Yeah, I get that all the time. Of course, he's a lot older than I am."

"Still, I've seen the documentaries. You look just like a young Charles Manson. It's uncanny."

"Just lucky I guess. Tell the truth, I make a little cash on the side as a Manson impersonator."

Without his awareness, a frown appeared on Murray's face. "Who wants a Manson impersonator? Who'd pay for that? Surely not advertisers."

"You're right. It's a very specialized niche. Mostly private parties attended by a very specific slice of the population, to put it politely. Then there's the occasional metal music video." Daniel laughed and made a dismissive gesture with one hand. "But, you're not here to talk about me. Am I right?" He did not wait for an answer. "You, Mr. Murray Gebhardt, are here to receive an educational upgrade."

Murray nodded. "Well, to learn about it anyway. You're highly recommended by Harrison, but I have a few questions."

Daniel's chair squeaked as he leaned back and kicked his right foot up onto his desk top. He touched the fingertips of both hands together in, what seemed to Murray, a delicate gesture.

"Ask away, my friend."

"Well, to start with, I couldn't find your company," he referred to the card for the one hundred and second time, "Mind Expansion Enterprises, in any of the usual continuing education listings."

Daniel's head bobbed affably behind the pyramid of fingertips. "Yes, I'm sure that's true. We get our clients pretty much exclusively by word-of-mouth."

Murray cleared his throat. "Uhm…naturally, I'm curious about your credentials."

With an aggravated squeak from the chair, Daniel leaned forward aiming both index fingers at Murray. "Our credentials are impeccable. The only credentials worth a damn are results. Am I right?"

"Yes…" Murray's reply was tentative; some part of him was desperately clinging to his skepticism.

"Unless we accomplish exactly what we promise, my friend, you do not pay a dime."

Murray nodded, pursing his lips. Things were sounding good. Still, he considered himself a shrewd consumer and he wanted to keep it that way.

"I'm sure Harrison told you our program is not for everyone. That's why I had you allot two hours of your time, so we can talk things over and figure out if Mind Expansion Enterprises is a good fit for you. Hungry?"

The question took Murray by surprise. He opened his mouth, but before he could speak, Daniel continued.

"I like to take my clients to lunch. Usually, over the course of a lunch conversation, I can make an assessment. I pick up the tab. Lunch costs you nothing. You like sushi?"

Murray drew a critical breath into one side of his mouth.

"Okay, sushi's not your thing," Daniel said, not missing a beat. "You a health food guy? Salad bar sound like the ticket?" Murray's expression was all the answer the man needed. "Great. I'll drive. Just let me lock the front door."

After locking up at 4315 Granada Street, they got in a surprisingly nice Mercedes and headed east. After a couple miles, they passed under a freeway overpass and into a much nicer community on the edge of the international airport. Daniel pulled into the driveway of a very nice hotel and stopped at the valet parking kiosk. The valet approached smiling the smile of a service employee who recognizes a good tipper.

"Daniel, my man," he exclaimed, jumping right into a multi-part handshaking ritual which Murray found a bit confusing. "Who's your friend?"

"This is Murray," Daniel said, handing the man his keys. "Murray, this is Link. Not so much the missing kind, but short for Lincoln."

"Good to meet you, Murray," Link called over the top of the Mercedes, a prominent gold tooth flashing in the afternoon sun.

"Likewise," Murray answered.

Daniel wasted no time heading for the revolving door that led into the hotel lobby. Murray followed as Link whipped the car out of the circular drive toward the parking garage.

On the other side of the revolving door, Daniel hesitated long enough for Murray to arrive at his side. "Good kid, Link. He's one of our graduates."

Murray looked over his shoulder, trying to imagine what a man like Link would have learned at Mind Expansion Enterprises. But, when he turned back Daniel was disappearing into a restaurant off the lobby. A few minutes later they were seated in a booth, each with a heaping plate of salad. Murray spread Italian dressing methodically over his and began cutting the salad into bite-sized chunks. Daniel dumped a couple of ramekins of bleu cheese dressing onto his mountain of greenery and shoveled a generous forkful into his mouth. He washed it down with iced tea and said, "Okay, so what is it exactly you need to learn, Murray?"

"Chinese."

"That's easy enough. Which dialect?"

"I don't know." The question made Murray self-conscious. "I guess I thought you'd tell me which one I needed. Whatever they speak in Beijing."

"Beijing Mandarin. Easy. It's not like you need to learn brain surgery or advanced physics. That's good. Those things are a bit harder, more expensive."

Murray stared at the man across the table, a mouthful of salad stabbed on the end of his fork. "You mean you could teach me those skills if I wanted to learn them?"

"Of course. Just a matter of acquiring the sources." Daniel stared at Murray as he chewed enthusiastically on another mouthful of salad. After he'd swallowed and gulped more tea, he said, "The more common a skill, the easier it is for us to plug you in. Fortunately for you, there were several billion Chinese-speaking individuals last time I checked." He allowed himself a short laugh, then picked at a bit of lettuce between his teeth. "How much exactly did Harrison tell you about our method?"

"Nothing really. I suppose he thought you'd explain it to me."

"Okay," Daniel set his fork aside and leaned back in the booth. "Tabula Rasa. Good. Let me fill you in. First, you might not think it to look at me, but I have a PhD in Psychology." Murray nodded, nipping salad from the end of his fork. "I'm well-versed in the academic models of modern psychology as they are currently taught. I know what they have to say about brain as opposed to mind, et cetera. I can tell you this," he jabbed an emphatic finger toward Murray, "most of what they're teaching in universities today is not at all aimed at helping the individual excel. Rather, it is more of a classification scenario aimed at helping the psychologist to label and control those placed under his scrutiny. Modern companies do not want a workforce full of individuals operating at their maximum potential. That sort of thing is far too intimidating for upper management. What they prefer are convenient ways to herd cattle so management doesn't have to worry about competition from the ranks. You follow me?"

Murray sipped his tea. "Yes, I believe I do."

"The Mind Expansion Enterprises origin story goes like this; one day," Daniel deftly continued explaining and eating, both with admirable speed, "as I was driving along in my car, listening to NPR, I heard a report that forever changed my outlook and my life. It seems there was a young man attending a pool party. After a few drinks, he carelessly dove into the shallow end of the pool and sustained a serious head injury. He was rushed to a hospital and in time fully recovered. But, there was an unexpected kink in this particular case. Even though he'd never had a single lesson or so much as expressed interest in learning to play the piano, the young man found he was suddenly able to perform like a concert virtuoso." Daniel stared at Murray letting his words sink in.

"How?"

"Exactly the question I asked. How could a man acquire previously unknown skills, skills of a very specific and highly developed nature, simply as a result of a head injury?" Daniel smiled thoughtfully, as if enjoying the recollection of his quest to find the answer. "I started with science. I interviewed every authority I could. Want to know what I learned?"

Murray nodded eagerly.

"Nothing. Zip. They couldn't tell me a damn thing. The paradigm under which they are operating doesn't allow for a guy to get conked on his noggin and suddenly play classical music on the piano like he's been playing since the age of three. They said it's impossible. But, we knew it wasn't impossible, because it had happened. They couldn't be bothered with the facts. They'd already made up their minds. I interviewed the very guy. Got a sworn affidavit from him. I heard him play the fucking piano! Beautiful! It was no hoax. My major breakthrough occurred when the guy told me when he was playing the piano, he sometimes felt as if someone else was using his body, his hands and fingers."

Murray noticed his mouth was dry. He sipped his tea. "If not a hoax, what was it?"

"A transmission."

"Hmm?"

"Sounds weird, doesn't it? It was what I call a transmission. Talk to any old school Tibetan about it and they'll totally agree with me. You see, the human brain is not the source of consciousness, nor even really the storehouse of information. Basically, it's like an antenna. Through this antenna we can receive and transmit information. I became convinced that the injury to the subject's brain enabled a transfer of skill, most likely from a disembodied entity."

Murray drew in a sharp breath. His expression clearly conveyed disapproval of the turn the explanation had just taken. "Disembodied entity?" His tone was desperately incredulous; something akin to fear appeared in his eyes.

"Before you get your panties in a wad, remember you don't pay a red cent unless we can transfer the desired skill, in your case Beijing Mandarin, to your conscious mind." Daniel swigged his tea, emptied the glass and signaled for one of the waiters to refill it. Turning back to Murray he said, "And don't worry. We don't have to bust your head to accomplish it. Relax. Let's finish our salads." With gusto, Daniel attacked the food before him. In a somewhat more timid fashion, Murray transferred salad from his plate to his mouth, glancing up to receive a reassuring wink from his host.

Back at Mind Expansion HQ, Daniel parked the Mercedes and led Murray to the front door. As he unlocked the door, Murray said, "Mind if I check on my car. No offense, but the neighborhood's a little sketchy."

"No offense taken. But, your inspection's unnecessary."

"I don't know. There were some kids just hanging out when I parked."

Daniel placed a firm hand on Murray's shoulder. "No one in this neighborhood will ever touch the property of one of our clients. Trust me."

"How can you be so sure?"

"They know better. For the moment, you'll have to take my word for it. But, I think you'll understand completely very soon now."

Daniel led the way to the end of the hall which turned to the right and ended at a set of double doors. He rapped on the door and a female voice answered, "Come in." Opening the door, he gestured for Murray to enter. The room was a large office full of furniture, an Oriental rug, brass and ceramic religious icons from all the world's major religions. A haze hung like morning smog over the chamber, swirling in mysterious eddies as they entered, rising in a serpentine column from a bowl of sand in which five or six sticks of incense were burning. Murray blinked, his eyes instantly irritated by the airborne particulates.

Seated on the sofa was an old woman smoking a cigar, her skin a leathery brown, her eyes dark and shining. A blue cloth was wrapped around her head; a long, colorful skirt draped her bony legs. She did not move, but stared intently at Murray. None of them spoke for a moment which threatened to go on for ever.

"What's she supposed to be?" Murray whispered to Daniel.

"She's not *supposed* to be anything. She *is* a gypsy and possessed of a very specific skill set from which you will soon profit." Daniel pushed past him and plopped down on a recliner. "Come on in, Murray. Murray this is Gloria. Gloria, meet our new client Murray."

Waving at the smoke, Murray moved to the chair on the opposite side of the rug.

"Yeah, the atmosphere's a little heavy, Gloria. I'm going to circulate some air."

"Suit yourself," said the gypsy. She eyed Murray and mashed her cigar out in a large ash tray on the coffee table at her feet.

"We gotta breathe," Daniel said, hopping up and going to a wall-mounted thermostat unit. He pressed a couple of buttons and a fan kicked on. Within a matter of seconds, much of the smoke had been sucked from the room. "Better?" he said, breathing deeply and looking to Murray for his approval.

"Thanks," Murray said, his eyes glued on the gypsy woman.

The woman leaned forward, placing her elbows on her bony knees, clasping her shriveled hands together. "You are Murray Gebhardt. You work for Gelco International and you want to acquire the ability to speak Beijing Mandarin."

"She's good, huh?" Daniel prompted.

"Come on, Daniel," Murray said, relaxing into his chair. "Let's get serious. She could've been listening to everything we said over lunch. If you want me to be impressed, you'll have to do better than that."

"The man wants to be impressed," Daniel said to Gloria, his eyes still on Murray. A smirk that suggested gloating formed on his lips.

The old woman closed her eyes. "You were born in Peoria. You attended Francis Busbee Elementary School. Your second grade teacher's name was Mrs. Holden. You had a crush on her. Your first real kiss was with a girl named Rebecca Downes at summer camp on Lake Watchobee. You lost your virginity to your next door neighbor's wife when you were sixteen. *That's* something you never told *anyone*. You're divorced, in a financial hole and you think the only way out of your money problems is to apply for the position in Beijing. You love your daughter Hannah and want to make sure she gets a good education." Gloria stopped talking, opened her eyes and scratched the back of her neck with one finger.

"Impressed yet?" Daniel asked.

Murray looked stunned, his mouth open, his eyes a bit glassy. He did not respond.

"Hello, Murray…" Daniel waved. "You still with us, bro? Or do we need to adjourn for a while until you come back to planet Earth?" He and the gypsy exchanged a knowing glance.

Murray nodded. "Okay. You got my attention."

"Good. Down to business. Gloria I'm sure Murray wants as unobtrusive a passenger as possible."

"Passenger?" Murray asked, weakly, still staring at Gloria. The woman returned his gaze with undisguised disdain.

"Yeah. That's what we call them, for want of a better term. Whatcha got, Gloria?"

The woman closed her eyes again. "I have a Buddhist monk. He just wants to be able to sit quietly and meditate on a daily basis."

"That sound okay to you, Murr?"

"Huh? What do you mean?"

"Yeah," said Daniel, "I forget. This isn't always obvious to everyone. Okay. The disincarnate entity who can help you speak Chinese is a Buddhist monk. In return for his services, he wants to be able to sit, *in your body*, for a certain amount of time each day and meditate. How's that sound?"

"I…I don't know."

"Come on, Murray. It doesn't get any better than this. Some of these guys want the moon. Believe me; you don't *even* want to know some of the negotiations we've made. I guarantee you; this is the easiest deal you're going to make."

"He also wants to visit a cherry orchard when the trees are blooming. Not every year, but as close to annually as possible," Gloria said, her eyes still closed.

Murray stared silently at the woman, then at Daniel. His head shook slightly from side to side. He looked confused.

"Listen, buddy," Daniel said, leaning back in his chair with a heavy sigh, "We can't move forward on this deal without your approval. Do you accept the terms or not?"

"I don't know. I just…"

"Look. Let's make this simple. How much is this deal worth to you? How much more money can you make if you get this job?"

Murray did not like discussing his personal finances with anyone.

"Come on, dude. Or do you want me to have Gloria pluck it out of your head?"

Oh. Yeah. He'd forgotten about that. "An extra hundred grand a year. Maybe more."

"So the question is; are you willing to let your passenger meditate daily and visit a cherry orchard once a year in exchange for that kind of money? Seems like a no-brainer to me."

"All right," Murray said at last.

"Good!" Daniel clapped his hands together and grinned like a madman. "Gloria, do your thing!"

The gypsy rose from the sofa and began muttering something, too low for Murray to make it out. He couldn't even say for sure if it was English. Still, it had a familiar ring to it. She tapped each of his shoulders as she circled his chair, saying her special words. After a minute or less, she took her seat on the sofa, picked up her cigar and lit it. With a sly smile she eyed Murray before blowing a silvery blue smoke ring toward the ceiling.

"Done deal." Daniel rose from his chair. "Thank you, Madame Gloria."

Gloria nodded, acknowledging his thanks.

"Come on, Murr. Just got some papers for you to sign." He placed a hand on Murray's shoulder and coaxed him up out of the chair. Murray moved like a man in shock, like maybe he'd just witnessed a terrible auto accident or had been informed that he only had six months to live.

Back in his office, Daniel said, "Its okay man. A lot of guys react the same way. It's a lot to get used to all at once. A whole new world. You want a drink? Might settle your nerves. I have some scotch."

Murray said nothing, just stared into space breathing slowly, his mouth hanging open. With a sudden movement, like a televangelist slapping the forehead of a petitioner, Daniel shoved him into a chair.

"What the hell?" The jolt aroused Murray from his stupor. He eyed the man standing over him with incipient anger.

Smiling, Daniel seated himself on the edge of his desk. "There's Murray. How you feeling, sport? Welcome back. Now, do you or do you not want a sip of scotch?"

"No. It's much too early." Murray stretched his arms nervously, tugging the cuffs of his shirt out of his jacket sleeves.

"Early, yes, but certainly there is cause for celebration. You, my friend, have a new skill which is going to increase your income by more than a hundred large. Sure you don't want that scotch? Might settle your nerves for the drive home."

"No…well, maybe."

"There you go! Wise decision. Just what the doctor ordered? Right? After all, you have undergone a significant change here." Daniel turned and opened the top drawer of his filing cabinet. From the drawer he withdrew a fifth of scotch whiskey and a couple of short glasses. "In an amazingly short amount of time you have had your world view radically altered." He poured a shallow pool of the amber fluid into each of the glasses. "It takes time to adjust." Daniel handed a glass to Murray and raised his own. "To the profitable and distinguished future career of Murray Gebhardt." He emptied his glass. Murray sipped, then cradled the glass close to his chest in both hands. "I'm concerned, Murr. Are you all right? I don't need to call an ambulance or anything, right?"

"No," Murray managed a mildly indignant response to the request. "I'm fine. Just give me a minute." He sipped again, letting the scotch burn some warm comfort all the way down to the pit of his stomach.

"Take all the time you need, my friend." Daniel circumnavigated his desk and plopped down into his chair, heaving a sigh and opening a drawer. He shuffled papers for a moment, then dropped a couple of stapled documents on the desk top, spinning them around to the proper reading position for Murray. "Look these over, if you like. A copy for you and one for our files. The standard agreement. It's all pretty straightforward. You can read it here or at your leisure when you get home. Feel free to call if you have any questions. I'm easy to reach."

Murray wet his lips with the scotch once more, leaning forward and taking his reading glasses from his coat pocket, he slipped them onto his nose and began reading. Daniel poured himself another splash of liquor and leaned back patiently. The plants on his window sill caught his eye, prompting him to rise from his chair and pluck a couple of unhealthy leaves from one of them. He dropped the leaves in his waste basket and resumed his seat, this time leaning forward over his desk, hands clasped, his face a mask of smiling, benevolent expectation.

Murray looked up from the document. "There's nothing here about what happens in the case of a default by either of us. There's nothing about location of jurisdiction governing the agreement."

Daniel couldn't suppress a laugh. "Murr, nobody defaults. The deal is done. Whether you sign the paper or not you're on the hook. You've been granted the ability to speak the Chinese language. In return you *will* pay the amount of money specified. We won't *default*; we've already given you what you want. You won't default, because you're a stand-up sort of guy. Right?"

Murray nodded nervously. "Sure, but..."

"No buts. Murray, if by some bizarre stretch you decided to not pay us, the matter goes to a higher court than you can find on this planet. It's automatic. Like I said, the deal's done. These papers are just to maintain some sense of the familiar for *your* benefit. We can toss them in the trash if you like. Makes no real difference."

"How do I know I can speak Chinese? I don't *feel* like I can." Murray shifted in his chair and raised the scotch to his lips.

"Good question. With languages it's a matter of becoming acclimated. Usually it kicks in when someone speaks to you in the other language. Find someone who speaks Beijing Mandarin and you'll be chatting up a storm before you know it. Pretty soon it'll seem like you've been speaking it all your life."

Sighing, Murray leaned forward and signed both copies of the agreement. Daniel nodded, leaned forward, affixed his signature to both and offered one to Murray. "One for you and one for our files." As Murray took the papers, Daniel stood and leaned over the desk with his hand extended. "Pleasure doing business with you, bro."

Realizing this was his cue to leave, Murray stood, draining the remainder of scotch from his glass. He placed the glass on the desk top and took Daniel's hand in his own. "Thank you."

Daniel pointed a finger at him when Murray released his hand. "I expect to hear great things from you, Murr."

The Golden Dragon was a little family-operated Chinese restaurant Murray had eaten in perhaps a dozen times. The people there knew him and always greeted him in a friendly manner. He'd often heard shrill cries issuing from the kitchen area as family members rebuked one another. Had the cries been Beijing Mandarin? He hoped so as he parked his car and entered the shadowy dining room. It was too early for the dinner crowd, too late for the lunch patrons. A young woman in her early twenties was seated behind the counter crunching numbers on a calculator. Her expression of mild irritation swiftly transitioned to a happy smile when she recognized him.

"Oh, you come very early today," she said, rising from her stool.

"Are you serving?" Murray asked her, a bit uncomfortable with deviating from his norm and having the deviation noticed by the woman. He wasn't hungry, but the matter simply would not wait until dinner time.

"Sure." She grabbed a menu and led him to the same booth where he always sat. "You want Green Tea?"

"Yes, that would be fine," he answered, sliding into the booth.

"You need a menu or will it be the usual? Egg Foo Young with shrimp, right?"

"Sounds good," Murray said, smiling up at the woman, realizing for the first time that he *always* ordered the same thing and appreciating the fact that she remembered it.

"Okay."

She turned and walked with child-like energy into the kitchen which lay behind a curtain of beads in a narrow doorway. He could hear her conversing in abrupt bursts of Chinese, sharp and seemingly aggressive with the older woman who worked there, probably her mother. Did he understand it? He wasn't sure. It felt a bit like the old one was saying, 'Who's here at this hour?' Then he felt like the young woman was saying, 'The older man who likes shrimp Egg Foo Young. The one who's nice, but not a great tipper.'

When the woman returned with his Green Tea, he mustered his courage and asked, "Do you speak Beijing Mandarin?"

"Mandarin?" The girl cocked her head, clearly puzzled as to why he would ask. "We speak Mandarin, yes."

Murray nodded. "Good." He wanted to say more, but he was feeling even more self-conscious than usual. Talking with women he found attractive was a bit of a challenge, even if it was a waitress in a humble Chinese restaurant. He coughed,

"Why do you ask about Mandarin? She asked him, staring in a sincere fashion and hugging the tray on which she'd transported the tea to her chest.

"Well, you see, I'm trying to learn Mandarin." Murray managed to hold a steady eye contact with the woman.

Her head drew back in a way that said, 'You're shitting me,' in any language.

"No. Really."

"What made you decide to learn Mandarin?" She asked, but not in English.

Without hesitation, Murray spoke, feeling as the words came out of his mouth like someone was pouring warm water over the crown of his head and that the warmth was slowly transferring through every cell of his body until it reached his toes. "I am applying for a position with Gelco International as a plant liaison in their Beijing facility. I intend to live there, perhaps for many years, so I must master the language."

The girl's narrow eyes widened so suddenly that the effect was comical. Murray could not avoid laughing. "You speak Mandarin so good! Why you never let me know before now?"

"Just self-conscious I guess. I didn't wish to appear foolish."

"You played a trick on me!" The young woman wagged a finger at him in mock anger, laughed delightfully and returned to the kitchen. As the beads chinked together from her passage, he could hear her excitedly explaining to her mother that he could speak perfect Mandarin.

"Oh," her mother answered cautiously. "We'd better not call him a cheap skate, then."

"Mother!"

Murray laughed to himself and determined to leave a generous tip. It was a good long while before the girl returned with his meal, but when she did she brought her mother and two brothers to the table so that all could hear him speak Mandarin with such elegance. They visited with him for several minutes, before departing to allow him to enjoy his meal. It seemed to Murray it was the most pleasant conversation he'd experienced for many years. Maybe even the best ever.

That night after a couple of glasses of red wine, Murray overcame his reservations and dialed Daniel's cell number. After several rings, he answered.

"Hello."

"Daniel, it's me, Murray Gebhardt."

"Murr! How's it hanging, mi compadre?" It seemed to Murray that Daniel had consumed more than a few alcoholic beverages himself. A woman said something in the background, to which Daniel responded, "Naw, it's a just a new client. Won't take a minute."

"Sorry for the interruption."

"No problem, bro. What can I do for you?"

"I just had to tell you, hell, I had to tell somebody, anybody that the operation was a success!" Murray's voice carried an enthusiasm that was not just unusual, in reality it had never before manifested.

"The operation is always a success, Murr. But, glad to hear it!"

Murray quickly ran down the events at the Chinese restaurant. Daniel was patient and generous with compliments. As the conversation was drawing to a close, Murray said, "I had just one more question. Something I've been wondering about."

"Shoot, my man! What is it?"

"The passengers… are they *always* disincarnate?"

There was silence on the line. Finally, Daniel said, "Murray, you dog, I knew you were smarter than you let on!"

"Well, I try."

"And you're asking this question because of the Charlie connection?"

"Yeah."

"No, they don't have to be dead. This deal with Charlie, it's harmless really. Hell, he's known forever that he'll never get out of prison. So, the thing I have going with him, just gives him a chance to get out and play once in a while."

"Play?"

"Yeah. Like I told you…private parties, music videos. To some people he's more of a celebrity than a criminal. Know what I mean?"

"I suppose."

"All in all it's a harmless thing. He plays, gets to feel free, have a little fun. You know, get drunk, high, whatever. It's not like it gets out of hand. Well, I mean…hardly ever…" ▲

Boxes of Dead Children

by Darrell Schweitzer

When the last of the workmen were done installing his "effects" into his new abode and the last of their trucks disappeared down the rough, gravel road, he really wished he could just blow up the little bridge that connected him with the rest of the world and become the most spectacular recluse since Howard Hughes. He pressed down, hard, on the imaginary plunger. *Boom!* The place was called Eagle's Head for some obscure reason, a little knob of land off the Maine coast at the end of a peninsula, amid tiny, rocky islands. High tides had washed away just enough that where he stood was an island now, too, but for that bridge, and if he could blow it up, well, all the better, because a gazillionaire minus his gazillions still has some resources left and he was sure he could continue to pay the private security firm he employed to float baskets of groceries over to him once a week and otherwise restrict access and leave him alone.

His was a name anyone would know, once a celebrity, the Boy Inventor (aged twenty-something), creator of _______, essential element in the daily lives of millions (who have to pay for it), the new Thomas Edison, who used to be in all the papers as an inspiration or perspiration of the American Dream, but was now, at sixty-something, if you believed hostile sources, the pirate entrepreneur who'd cheated his buddies out of _______, and was pursued by the slings and arrows of congressional investigations, not to mention a mysterious Woman in Red, several distraught ex-wives and former offspring—a.k.a. money-grubbing leeches—plus any number of lawyers, lawyers, lawyers, until he had made his way in abject retreat by swerve of shore and bend of bay to Eagle's Head, Maine, and a curiously long-vacant but "fully furnished" property which a Martha's Vineyard realtor who owed him a debt of discreet gratitude had managed to procure for him.

Boom.

He turned to regard his new acquisition, and the odd thought came to him that if aliens had beamed up bits and pieces of famous edifices from all over the world and glued them together at random, that would only begin to explain the architecture of this place, which had everything from Gothic towers to Romanesque windows to twirly Italianate pillars to a classic, wooden, late Victorian wooden porch on which one could enjoy the sea breeze.

It occurred to him a little later, as he sat on that porch in the evening, that he had so much privacy here that if he wanted to lounge about in a lion-skin loincloth while reading old Tarzan novels, he bloody well could, because amid his vast personal library he actually owned an expensive set of Edgar Rice Burroughs first editions he'd once picked up on a whim, and he did not doubt that the wardrobes inside contained a lion-skin or two; and besides, he was, despite his considerable falling-down in the world, still rich enough to be "eccentric" rather than merely mad, like that crazy DuPont before he'd finally shot somebody.

But a mosquito bit him, and then another, and another, something no amount of isolation or money could do anything about at this time of year, so he went inside. It was not loincloth weather.

Inside, the hallway, which the realtor had described to him as an "atrium," was filled with *stuff.* He was very much into *stuff,* things, objects of art or curiosity, which became a kind of expression of his mind, like graffiti written on the fabric of reality, to an extent more than one of his ex-wives had described as pathological: *stuff,* his own and that of his rather mysterious "fully furnished" predecessor who had built this little hideaway back in the days of Newport mansions, when anything smaller than the palace of Versailles was accounted a "cottage." He himself, the product of a simpler age, had grown up watching *The Addams Family* on TV and had always wanted to live in a house like that, and now, as nearly as possible, he did, complete with a stuffed bear, a samurai statue, and a two-headed concrete tortoise in the living room.

But there was something else here, too, something he couldn't quite define, some sense of an Other, no doubt caused by the presence of a good deal of antique *stuff* which was not his—*i.e.* which had not accumulated through the remembrances and associations of *his* life. The theory of *stuff* held that whoever lived in a bare, pristine apartment with no stuff in it was probably not worth getting to know. His predecessor must have been interesting, at least.

So what he was doing here was intruding into the lingering mind of *someone else*, hoping to fuse his own with it. The bronze and lacquer dragon clock in the atrium, or the life-sized, age-darkened, papier mache' bobble-head figure of a Chinese attendant had not been his, but they intrigued.

Concerning the former owner, who had left the place boarded up while his estate was left in suspended animation for decades, the realtor had said very little.

Boom. If only he could blow up every connection to the outside world and merely disappear into this place, into the woodwork and accumulations of the house itself. He had to admit to himself, when he had such thoughts, that he was tired, not young anymore, and there were so many things in the world he no longer cared about, most of which had lawyers attached.

But it wasn't as simple as that of course. No isolation can be perfect, particularly if you want modern conveniences. The electricity worked. It worked well enough when he found the electric train layout and followed an antique steam engine as it rattled across table-tops and over the lintel of a door, then through a hole cut in the wall, along a ceiling on a high ledge, up a spiraling staircase, one, two, three storeys, until it came to an attic room which had been laid out with an immense tabletop display of a rolling prairie, a station in the middle of it where the train came to a stop, and, stretching in all directions, hundreds of tiny gravestones, most of them with names written on them, but some still blank.

Then the power went out, and he was drawn naturally to the fading light of a window. He could see, across Penobscot Bay, a lighthouse in the distance, two or three sailboats beneath a darkening sky, and, below him, on what must be the back lawn, a single grave, a real one, in the back yard, surrounded by a fence.

He spared himself such clichés as *Well, that's weird,* and he didn't feel particularly afraid. He wasn't quite sure what he felt.

The oddest thing that came to him just then was the temptation, not to blow up his last bridge to the outside world, but to reconnect. So he pulled up a chair and sat down by the window, in the fading light, and got out his cell phone and turned it on. Yes, there was a signal here. He was online, before long fingering his way up and down the screen, reading news, wandering over the Facebook, and then he found a mention of himself in the form of a crudely Photoshopped image of his face on a devil's body with a wriggling boy and girl spitted on his pitchfork and a caption: IS IT TRUE THAT THE RICH EAT BABIES?

Before he could even turn the phone off a voice behind him in the room distinctly said, "That is not a good idea," and somehow the phone was snatched out of his hand.

He turned around in alarm and said, "Who's there?" but of course there was no one there, just the shadow-filled room with the strange train layout and the tiny graveyard.

That the place should be haunted only seemed appropriate. If it were not, he should call the realtor and ask for a discount.

Call him with what? His phone was gone.

He must have dropped it. He could come up here in daylight, with a flashlight if necessary, and search for it.

Then he'd have a long talk with the ghost. Maybe the two of them could become friends, and commiserate without fear of wiretaps and lawsuits.

He realized this was not a normal reaction, but then, he was not here to be normal.

This was well beyond the level of lion-skin loincloths, something deeper than mere eccentricity.

He tried to open himself to the influence of the house, as he explored room after room, some filled with old furniture, shelves crammed with newspapers, another crammed with plaster, life-sized figures of clowns, yet another with every inch of wall space covered with very old, dusty, mounted heads of birds and animals, including what might have been a pterodactyl. Often it was hard to see, because the power was off. Sometimes he just groped. Once he thought he was running his hands over a mummy case. It smelled of wood and exotic spices. Splinters came off on his fingertips. But he could see nothing until he finally found yet another winding staircase which took him down to the kitchen.

Just then the lights came on.

It was quite a modern kitchen, refurnished and stocked as he had instructed. He opened the freezer, got out a frozen entrée and popped it in the microwave, which cheerfully chirped at him as he pressed the bottoms.

He resisted the temptation to actually turn the television on.

As he ate his meager dinner in silence, his hand drifted over to a large book that lay on the table, an album of some kind. He opened it, and saw that it was indeed a late 19th century photo album, each of the pictures in a stiff cardboard setting hinged with cloth, all black & whites of course, some of them badly faded, a couple of them tintypes and one on glass.

They were all pictures of children, the boys in stiff suits or even sailor suits, and short pants, their socks neatly drawn up to their knees, the girls in frilly dresses and bonnets. It took him a while as he turned the pages, from photo to photo, to figure out what was wrong with their faces, their blank expressions. A couple of them seemed to be wearing round, smoked glasses, or else they had pennies on their eyes.

They were dead, all of them. He knew that it had once been the custom to photograph the dearly departed one last time, and so such pictures did exist, and a whole album of them like this was a fascinating, if decidedly morbid—and no doubt very valuable—collector's item; but, still, as he came to this conclusion, he snapped the book shut. He laid his fork down gently. He reached for the TV remote.

And then the power went out again.

"You have your little hobbies. I have mine."

Now he actually was alarmed, but at something more mundane than a ghost.

"Who the hell's there? Who's there?"

He groped around in a drawer. He found a steak knife. Armed with this, he turned to face the darkness threateningly.

"I *said*, who the hell's there?"

There was no answer. He heard only faint creating and snapping. Old houses "settled," he knew. Maybe it was windy out. Maybe there were branches scraping against windows.

Knife in hand, he made his way around the kitchen, tapping things with the tip of the knife the way a blind man would with a cane.

There actually was a small flashlight in one of the drawers.

"I *said*, who—"

He flicked on the flashlight then jumped back as the beam revealed a face, right in front of him, but then he realized it wasn't a face at all, but a framed oval-shaped photo on the wall, of a man in a stiff collar and a suit, but whose face was somehow indistinct, and becoming even more indistinct by the moment, fading away as he watched.

He turned off the light. He briefly considered that maybe flashlights were bad for old photographs.

And while he stood there in the dark, he considered his options, some of which were, he knew, very traditional in a situation like this. They included:

Running screaming into the night.

Or making his way to the master library upstairs by candlelight and spending the evening poring over ancient, blasphemous, eldritch, forbidden, and crumbling tomes in arcane languages (which he would somehow be able to read), until he had ventured into truly forbidden territory which sufficiently altered his mind that he was no longer even remotely sane and all the more willing to invite in tentacular spooks from outer space, while incidentally discovering in a climax of mind-blasting horror what precisely the former owner of this house (of sinister repute, both the owner and the house) had been up to.

Calling in a team of professional ghost busters with their instruments and their technobabble, which would ultimately lead them to yadda-yadda—see, previous paragraph.

Going out into the back yard and digging up that grave with his *bare hands*.

Or just lying out there and listening to the voices from out of the ground.

Or waiting for the power to come back on and then watching TV. Something he could relate to, like *Big Bang Theory*, because he, too, was an awkward genius that nobody understood. This option included calling out for pizza, even if it was quite a ways for a delivery. First he'd have to find his phone.

Or none of the above.

What actually did happen after that was a little hard to follow. For one thing, he lost track of time. It was dark. It stayed dark. He wondered if the sun would ever rise. He thought he remembered distinct instances of sleeping, on a couch, or in a huge, canopied bed, and of getting up several times to go to the bathroom—fortunately the plumbing worked, even if the electricity didn't, and he laughed and repeated to himself the old joke in a comic-geezer's voice about, *I have an old man's bladder. Imagine how upset he was to discover it missing.* But it was still dark, and more than once he made his way down to the kitchen by candlelight and ate whatever he could find that didn't require cooking. And always, he avoided looking at the photo on the wall, or any of the ones in the album.

Now what was interesting was that he had the distinct sense that it was *his* album, and he began to remember how he had taken those photographs, one by one, and under what circumstances, which was very odd indeed, because he hadn't taken them. He, the inventor and entrepreneur and the subject of rude Photoshopped pictures on Facebook had done nothing of the sort, and those weren't digital photographs anyway. He had no idea how to use the sort of antique equipment that must have been employed in the creation of those pictures, even if, during his ruminations, he had found a whole room full of cameras and metal basins and bottles of chemicals.

Once he actually heard someone knocking loudly at the front door. He saw the gleam of headlights in the driveway. But he didn't answer it. That was for someone else, in another time.

He hadn't come here to be normal, he kept telling himself.

Time to break out the old loincloth and go swinging through the vines.

But that was not what he did—this not being loincloth weather—as he made his way slowly upstairs, through rooms filled with his own *stuff*, glimpsing by candlelight his comic-book collection, his movie posters, the glass case containing the Aurora model kits of the Frankenstein Monster and Dracula he'd built as a kid—as he was the sort of person who went through life *accumulating,* never letting go of anything—then into another room filled with his trophies, for innovation, for excellence, for making lots and lots of money and keeping most of it from anybody else—and after that the room full of stuffed, mounted heads, which brought back to his consciousness like bright bubbles of memory rising from a dark pool the vivid recollections of how exactly he had killed each one of these creatures. And yes, the pterodactyl was a joke, a clever fabrication given to him by a friend one Christmas after he'd returned from an expedition to Mato Grosso in 1922 and they'd both sat up reading aloud passages from *The Lost World* and getting a jolly good laugh over it. He found a closet filled with old suits and put one on, because a gentleman, even at home, had to maintain a certain standard. His fingers seemed to know what to do with the stiff, detached collar, even if his mind didn't.

He was a gentleman, despite some of the things that went on in that room filled with cameras and metal basins and sinks, and even though they didn't involve, exclusively, photography.

There was a room of knives. The walls were covered with them, each in little sheaths. Thousands of them.

And then it seemed that he was riding in the passenger car of a train, the steam engine whistling and roaring, as he gazed out the window past a landscape that seemed to twist over tabletops and along the lintel of a door and through tunnels and up spiraling flights of stairs until he found himself disembarking at the final stop, which was an old-fashioned wooden train station in the middle of an impossibly flat landscape covered with perfectly regular gravestones as far as he could see.

At the same time he was in the room where the toy train's track came to its terminus, where moonlight streamed in through a window, and he heard the sound of a foghorn from across the bay. Why would they blow a foghorn on a moonlit night? He wasn't sure, but they did.

"Choo! Choo! End of the line!" someone said.

"Who the *hell* is there?"

"We have our little hobbies. Wanna see?"

He followed, by candlelight, as the Other led him to a higher loft, the true attic of this part of the house, a long, low room under the eaves, and for just a moment what he saw looked, impossibly and absurdly, like something he'd seen in the dark once in that scenic metropolis of Shell Pile, New Jersey, a soft-shell crab farm out in the middle of a field, consisting of row upon row of rectangular tanks stacked on top of one another in a metal framework. But these were not tanks. They were boxes, white cardboard boxes, like gift boxes, the kind you'd get a doll or new suit in, carefully stacked row upon row on metal shelves.

"Look."

None of the boxes had lids. Inside each, surrounding by crumpled wrapping paper the way a new doll might be wrapped, lay the corpse of a child. He knew each of them. He remembered them. He knew their names. He had gently placed pictures of every one of them into his album.

Now some of them were starting to shrivel up or blacken, which made him sad, because he remembered how beautiful they had been.

But no, he argued, *he* hadn't done any of this. That was someone else. It was as if his memories and that of some *Other* were getting all mixed up now, but he was sure, no, that he had never been in this room before the *Other* had tricked him into it; and that was *not* his own picture on the wall in the kitchen with a face that faded away; and the children in the boxes did *not* call out to him and demand to know why? Why? Why did you hurt me? He hadn't hurt anyone. They were having such fun. Like the joke with the pterodactyl was such fun. *No one* asked him *Well, what about that guy you buried in the Pine Barrens near Shell Pile?* And he did not have to explain, as one might to a child, that to get where he had gotten, much less to hold onto what he had obtained, whether it be a perfect Aurora model kit of Dracula or a million dollars in hoarded rare gold coins that nobody else knew about, much less his legendary gazillions in the stock of ___, well, sometimes you have to do things that just have to be done, however unpleasant; so no one asked him about the fire in the sweatshop in Bangladesh either, and no one even said, *Who do you think you are kidding? Do you really think you can just hide away from the world and from the past forty years of your life with your head in the fucking sand? That doesn't work very well for ostriches either.*

That's not a good idea.

Good? Bad? He knew that he was not a bad man, and who was to judge anyway? Some things were beyond judgment.

He ran out of the loft, back down into the lower part of the attic, where the toy train was, where he could see a distant lighthouse out a window across the bay, and somehow, miraculously, his phone was right there, by the chair, where he'd dropped it, still on and glowing.

The last good idea he had involved scooping up that phone off the floor and pressing in a number he knew. His youngest daughter. He hadn't spoken to her in a very long time. He sensed, he hoped, that she didn't hate him quite as much as everybody else. If only he could just speak to her—

"That's not a good idea," the Other said.

"Yes, it's a very good idea!" he said, "a very good idea."

The phone was ringing.

"A very good idea!"

"Daddy? Is that you? What's a good idea?"

"I don't know," he said, and then he couldn't think of anything more to say.

Someone took the phone out of his hand and threw it across the dark room.

But of course there was no one in the room with him. He was standing there, alone, wearing an old-fashioned suit, and in the upper loft were boxes and boxes of dead children, whose names he knew.

* * * *

Later, there was a loud knocking at the door and he looked out another window and he saw the policemen down there in the driveway, and he laughed at the ridiculous jalopies they'd come in and the absurd uniforms they wore, like something out of an old, silent movie, but he knew they'd never find him, because he was here now and he was part of the house and he could just fade into the darkness until they'd gone away.

"Boom," he said. ▲

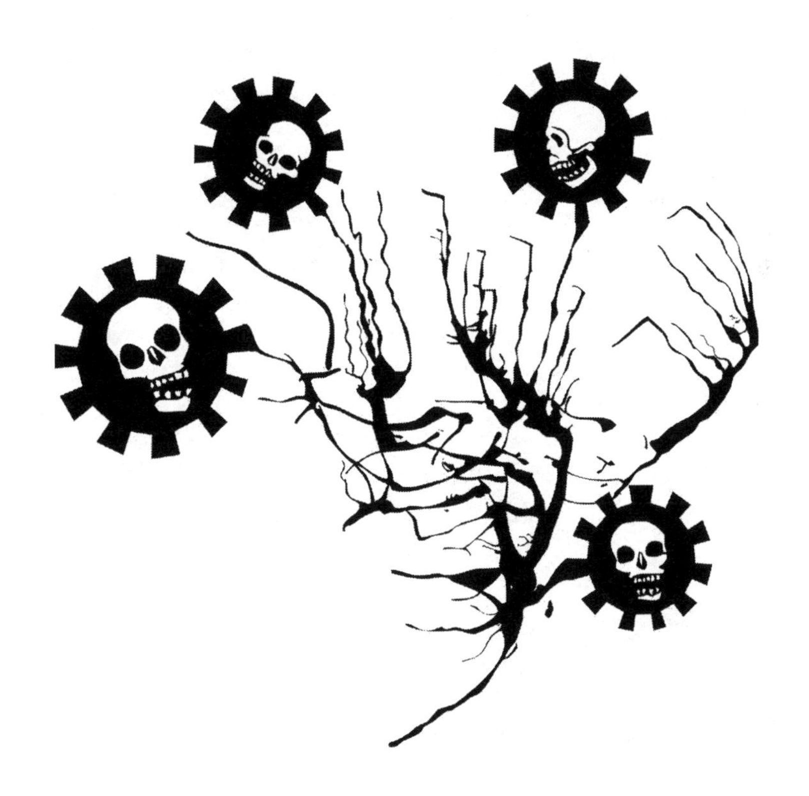

The Forgotten

by D.C. Lozar

Jake ripped the paper out of his notebook and crumpled it into a tight wad. The evening drizzle was getting serious, and splattering droplets had smeared much of what he had written. The writing exercise had been to describe a place that held special meaning to him. He sat on an overturned metal bucket with his back against the dead fig tree. Lightning had long ago split its trunk in two, and its charred branches offered little shelter from the rain. He tried again to imagine what his parents must have been like on their first date under this tree. He thought he heard them in the gentle rumble of thunder. He squinted, trying to see them in the twilight shadows. Rain blurred his vision, and he felt a lump forming in his throat.

He was not going to start crying. He hadn't wept when they died, and no stupid assignment was going to make him start. Jake wondered why he had come here. He could have stayed in his room and written from memory. It was his birthday, and he was acting like a baby.

An icy breeze blew across his neck and sent a chill down his back. If he didn't get inside soon, he was going to catch a cold. He slid his notebook, his pencil, and the wad of paper into his backpack. They would be worried about him. He should go back. Still, Jake stayed on his metal bucket and stared at the crumbling homes that lined this forgotten park. Boarded windows and locked doors didn't keep the ghosts out. The rain fell heavier now. His toes squished inside his sneakers as he stood up.

Raindrops clanged against the overturned bucket, echoing the hollow feeling in his chest. He turned to face the splintered trunk that had been the heart of the fig and wondered if he would ever be able to see it the way his parents had described it. When they told him bedtime stories, his favorites had always been about this tree. This spot was where they fell in love, where they had decided to have him, and where he had played in the grass as a toddler.

Since his parents died, Jake had learned that happy endings didn't happen. He had learned about social services, government run homes, and how most people didn't care if it was your birthday. Jake missed being held. He missed being loved and most of all he missed being wanted.

His therapist said he needed to explore these feelings, to write them down, and to start with a positive memory.

A flash of light and the deep growl of thunder pulled him back to the present. Jake hugged himself with shivering arms and took a step down the garbage littered path toward his new temporary home. It was dark now, and the trail was muddy. He hoped he could remember his way back. He took another step and something made him stop. He had forgotten something important that he couldn't leave behind. He stopped and thought as the rain rolled down his face.

What had he forgotten?

He had his notebook, pencil and backpack. But there was something else he needed.

He turned back toward the tree to see if he had left something, and he felt his feet go out from under him in the slippery mud.

The fall seemed to take a very long time. He felt a crack that sounded as loud as thunder and felt a pain swim up his leg that made him scream. It hurt worse than anything. Tears rushed to his eyes and were washed away by the rain.

Crying, he tried to sit up. Something was very wrong with his leg. His foot was going the wrong way. He tried to catch his breath. In an emergency, you weren't supposed to panic. He had to think clearly and develop a plan. He had broken something. No one knew where he was because he had snuck out. It was dark, too dark. He was sitting in a puddle. His underwear felt gushy. He shivered.

The rain played a sad melody against the old pail, drawing his attention. The fig tree was a dark shadow, its gnarled branches reaching for him like claws. Why had he come here?

Something moved. There was something in the night, in the storm, and it was coming up the path. Jake covered his eyes and squinted. He was scared. Should he call for help or try to hide? He heard voices. They sounded familiar, and they were calling for him.

"Jake!" a woman's voice called, worried and tired. "Are you out here?"

"Come on, Jake," complained a man's voice. "It's miserable out. Tell us where you are."

He tried to yell to them, but his voice was hoarse from the pain and all that came out was a groan. He thought about waving, but he needed his hands to stay upright.

"Every time he runs away, he comes back to this tree. If he's not here, we'll have to call for help."

"I still don't know how he got past me."

"His therapist said he might act out. They've been dredging up some old memories," said the woman. "He misses his family."

"Sometimes it's just better to forget the past, you know?"

The woman's flashlight swept over the tree, the pail, and then stopped. "Oh, my God."

Jake tried to shield his eyes from the light. His arm went out from under him, and his torso slid back into the mud. He howled at the pain in his leg.

Warm hands grasped his neck, lifting it, supporting his head. The woman had deep blue eyes, and Jake smelled vanilla perfume. He tried to remember her name. A green golf umbrella moved over them and blocked out the rain.

"Did you fall? Are you hurt?" There was concern in the woman's voice.

"I forgot something," he choked out the words. He was so glad they found him. He didn't even care if he got in trouble.

"I think he broke his leg." A middle-aged man in a bright yellow coat came into view. Jake had played cards with him. He was funny. "Put my coat over him. I'll get help."

Heavenly warmth enveloped Jake as they laid the yellow rain slicker over his chest. It smelled of cigarettes and coffee, but Jake loved it. His leg still throbbed, but the pain was better now that someone had found him. He watched the storm swallow the man.

"We should have been watching you closer." The woman tucked the corners of the raincoat around his shoulders and laid his head in her lap. She ran her warm fingers through his hair and moved it out of his eyes. Her face was kind. "Does it hurt?"

"I was trying to do the assignment, but I couldn't remember what the tree looked like."

"I know, dear. That's why you always come back here. Just rest. Sam went to get help."

Sam. Jake smiled. He remembered Sam.

Jake felt warmer now. The shivering stopped. The metal bucket rang out a happy pitter-patter song. He didn't feel bad about coming anymore. He had wanted to see the tree.

But what had he forgotten? Why had he turned back?

"It's my birthday today."

"I know. Did you like the cake?"

Jake nodded, but he couldn't remember it. Had they sung for him? Had he liked it when people he didn't know sang?

"It was a pretty special day wasn't it?" She patted his shoulder and smiled. "I mean, not everyone can live as long as you."

A flash of lightning burned an afterimage of the fig tree into Jake's mind. He could see it then, his metal walking cane, the thing he wasn't supposed go anywhere without.

He had forgotten how much he needed it.

Jake cried. ▲

Coffee with Dad's Ghost

Jessica Amanda Salmonson

My dad came to see me last night in a dream. I was sitting in a coffeehouse reading a University Press monograph on Japanese silent movies, lightly penciling notes in the margins of the hefty tome. I was thinking, "This has got to be a dream. But don't I actually own this book? I wonder where I put it."

At first I didn't recognize him as who expects to see their dad so many years after he's dead. And he was so much younger than when last we hung out. His hair was slicked back and he looked like a member of the Sharks or the Jets.

He had a cigarette between two fingers, unlit, as there's no smoking indoors; I bet that surprised him. Coffee without a cigarette. The rest of the pack was rolled up in a shirt sleeve, partly I suspect to show some of his tats.

"This coffee cost eight bucks," he said. "What the fuck?"

"Well, times have changed," I warranted.

He sat down, hung the unlit cigarette on his lower lip, where it flopped up and down as he talked. Though he was unexpectedly young, those were the same pale blue eyes. He'd been a good looking old fart. As a young man he was splendid, in a greaser sort of way. "Did you know all the faggots go to Hell?" he said. "The whole place is fabulous."

"I heard that joke."

"But you know what surprised me most of all? Satan's only about two feet tall. No shit. Mean little bugger. Always mad about something. But it's God he's really mad at. Or that's my theory. I've got considerable rank. Even earned some vacation time, so thought I'd drop by."

"Do you ever see Lumchuan?" I asked.

That brought out the sad-eyed look. "I never do," he said, adding wistfully, "She was a good woman."

I wanted to say, "Indeed she was. Always wondered why it was you of all her choices." But unexpectedly I was in my Forester driving on a dirt road through a clear-cut. There were wild blueberry bushes springing up everywhere with dangly white bellflowers.

I looked around to see if my dad was still with me, but I was alone. I suppose he was standing outside Starbucks with his cigarette lit finishing his coffee. I woke up in bed and immediately thought, "Dad has rank? Fuck me." ▲

Missed It By That Much

by Gregg Chamberlain

He looked outside and for the first time in his heart, Martin now truly saw the world as it was, and now would forever be. And he wept.

The End.

Nelson's fingers rested for a moment on the keyboard after typing in those final two words. He looked at them, clear, clean and comforting in Times New Roman 14-point solid black typeface on the white computer screen. He smiled.

"I did it," Nelson said, quietly. He did a quick save and closed the story file for *Where Zombies Go to Die*. "I did it," he repeated, a little louder now.

Nelson popped the storage flashdrive out of the USB port. He held it up in one hand and regarded it with wonder. "I did it!" He spun around in the chair at his cramped work station. "I honest to God *did it*!"

He punched the air. "Just some Zane Grey-wannabe hack, am I, Mike? Can't write anything but cheap western knockoffs, huh?" He held the flashdrive up towards the cheap tile ceiling. "In your face, man, 'cause this little breakout horror masterpiece will make me the next Stephen King, my dear doubting deadbeat brother-in-law."

Drive clutched tight in one hand, Nelson leaped up from the chair, bolted out of the tiny basement alcove that served as his writing room, and bounded up the stairs.

"Janine!" he called. "Honey, I've done it! I've written the very best, the most absolutely PERFECT zombie apocalypse novel!"

He burst out through the basement door into the kitchen. "Janine? Where are you?"

No sign of his wife anywhere in the kitchen. There was a wonderful spaghetti sauce smell wafting from a crock pot on the counter. But no Janine.

He heard a sound from the living room. "Janine?"

Nelson stepped over to the living room entry way and stood there, staring in shock at the scene before him. His wife, Janine, lay sprawled in the centre of the room, her long red hair spread out in a crimson fan on the carpet, its fibres already stained dark from the blood pooling beneath her head. Crouched over her, gnawing on the top of her skull, was Mr. DelVecchio, the postman.

Mr. DelVecchio looked up, bits of bone and bloody hair hanging from his black lips. "Brrrraaaaiiiinnnnssss?" Nelson heard the undead creature say.

The moaning zombie lurched up and staggered, arms outstretched, towards Nelson, Right into the path of an ornamental art-deco ashtray stand that Janine had bought at a flea market. Nelson snatched up the ashtray stand where it stood beside the entryway, swung it in a looping overhand arc, and smashed the sharp pointed corner of the solid metal base deep into Mr. DelVecchio's skull.

The zombie collapsed, dead again. Janine's body began to twitch. Nelson stepped over the dead zombie. He looked down as his wife's now-dull eyes opened. He lifted up the ashtray stand and swung it down again onto her head.

Nelson took a moment to bend down and pass a hand over Janine's face, closing her eyes again. Then he walked in a daze to the open front door and looked outside at the chaos now ruling the once-quiet neighbourhood street of their Ladner home. He closed the door without a word, turned the door lock and set the deadbolt.

He walked out of the living room, stepping over both of the bodies on the floor, and crossed back through the kitchen. Still carrying the ashtray stand, he went down the basement stairs and into his writing alcove. He sat down in front of the computer and let the ashtray stand drop to the floor beside the chair.

Nelson looked at the flashdrive still clutched in his other hand. He sighed. Tossed it onto the desk.

Well, crap, he thought. *That* market's tapped out now.

For a long moment after that non sequitur thought, Nelson sat staring at the black screen. Then he straightened. He woke up the computer, and inserted an empty drive. Opening a file, he started tapping on the keyboard.

APACHE JUSTICE

CHAPTER ONE

"Write what you know," muttered Nelson. "Write what you know. He continued tapping on the keyboard.

> High noon and the dusty main street of Laredo was empty, and quiet. Too quiet…

A Clockwork Muse

by Erica Ruppert

Clumsy with pain, she is borne down by the weight of her own fractured thoughts. Light glares. Unformed, unfocused, she cannot link one perception to another. Minutiae pick her apart. She is trapped in the details, present and past transparencies overlaid to create a cloudy mass where there is no yesterday, no before, only now, and now, and now, neverending. She clings to what she can.

Eventually the pain eases, resolves itself into the stretching of her muscles, the beating of her hollow heart. Sensation, inexplicable. She believes she knows what it is. Her mind locks it into its place. There, now. It is real.

She is aware of a childhood, but she cannot hold it. The memory slips. Automata have no past. She knows she is a construct, an imitation of a life cobbled together from borrowed memories. They are all true. She remembers sitting in a field in the July sun, waiting for her mother to spread the picnic blanket. She remembers the slow ache of arthritis in her hands when she shoveled the winter's first heavy snow. She is fragmentary and erratic in her recollections but convinced of them all the same. They are in her, loose as fallen leaves, and each is real.

But she is not. Her eyes are green glass, windows into the illusion of her soul. The man standing in front of her sees what he wants in them. He has imagined her into being, shaped her and done the fine work of her machinery. What rare elements did he use to assemble her, his Galatea, his Eve: platinum wires, slick titanium joints, silicon, smooth pale lab-grown skin through which the shadow of her composite skeleton can be seen. She is breathtaking, inhuman, flesh over plastic bones. She breathes.

"Delia," he says. "Come here."

She walks gracefully, as if she had always stood erect on her narrow feet, balanced her mass against gravity's subtle pull.

His name is Stephen. She already knows it.

His hands on her shoulders, running lightly down her arms. She feels it. She trembles, gooseflesh rising, alive.

He assesses her. She stands still, unsure, expectant.

"Fine," he says. "You are fine."

Feminine, she reaches up to smooth her hair.

Szmenski steps around Stephen, leans close to her and places his hand over hers, following her motion. "Yes," he says. "You are fine." She knows his name as well. She glances at Stephen, the need to do so innate.

Stephen's mouth twitches but he stands aside to let Szmenski scrutinize her.

Her hands are restless. She picks at her nails, running her fingers around the edge of them over and again.

"Stop it," Stephen says. "You'll ruin them."

Szmenski gently pulls her fingers apart. "Relax, Delia. There is no need to fret," he says.

He guides her hands to her sides, poses her like a demure mannequin.

"You are quite talented, Stephen. Delia, thank you."

Szmenski steps back to allow Stephen close to her again. His breath moves loose strands of her dark hair. She has no sense of him.

"Thank you, Doctor," Stephen says, never looking away from her. Just past his ear Delia sees Szmenski slide open a panel and leave them to themselves. She remembers.

* * * *

Beside Stephen in the quiet darkness, she wonders. Synapses fire, electricity jumps the gaps, makes its circuit. She thinks time may be passing. She remembers sunrise. Her head is full of stars.

* * * *

He leads her to a seat before the window, positions her at an angle to the light. He tilts her chin up and away from him. She looks over her shoulder at the clear blue sky.

"Stay like that," he says, retreating across the room. He picks up paper and charcoal, sketches her outline quickly before going back to fill in details. There are many portraits of her in the house, the bulk of them with her face tilted away, as though Stephen is wary of capturing all of her.

She is curious. She lingers over the sensation of her neck extended, the pull of the muscles. Outside, leaves rustle in the wind.

There is a flicker in her memory, in her vision. She can see herself sitting there. She remembers seeing it. She feels as if she is falling. Her limbs do not match her perception. She loses her pose, turning back to Stephen with her lips parted, already asking.

"What is it now, Delia? I told you to stay still." He is angry with her. She is finite, she is lacking. She is not what he wants, right now.

* * * *

Szmenski comes and goes. Sometimes he speaks to them, genial small talk about the day that reveals nothing; other times he watches quietly from a seat in the studio as Stephen paints. Delia has the feeling that she remembers him from before, but she has no before. His presence slots in among all the other pinpoints of memory.

* * * *

Stephen poses her again, this time standing with her hands pressed together palm to palm, fingers brushing her chin. She remembers praying, fervently. Clean tears spring up in her eyes. She does not know why. The mood fades. She dislikes modeling for Stephen, is subtly shamed by the multiple versions he makes of her. He has not yet begun this repetition, is still preparing his palette. She searches for other distractions.

There is a fine tear in her skin along the edge of her thumbnail. She picks at it until she can pinch it up and pull it back. She peels her hand like an orange. She is vaguely expecting pain, and blood, but it does not hurt. She is not surprised by the lacework of wires and slim rods revealed by her picking. She keeps going, stripping the skin from her arm in a long sleeve.

"Delia!" Stephen cries.

He reaches for her, crushing the metal bones of her hand in a hard grip as he stops her.

Without the skin to conduct sensation, she is only aware of pressure. She pulls her hand away, watching the slide and flex of her machinery.

"Don't touch anything. We have to fix this," Stephen says.

"I don't want it fixed. Not yet," she says.

"You can't stay like this," he says, already moving away.

* * * *

She remembers leaping from the cliff's edge into the cold deep pool. She landed badly, slamming into the water's surface before it gave in to her weight and let her sink. This stings like that did, like a raw electric current across her chest and belly. She jumps away from it, fearing the drowning that will follow.

"It's okay," Szmenski says, calm as air.

The needle glints and sparkles as it threads her skin back together. There is pain, but it is not hers. Still, she flinches.

"Be still, Delia," says Szmenski.

Her body relaxes. His hands are familiar, the slow process of reconstruction has happened before. She watches his hands move across hers, the delicate stitches he leaves behind. It will heal into scars so pale they will lay like lace on her skin. Ghosts of what will be. She remembers it.

Szmenski is always the one to put her back together. He has never allowed Stephen that privilege. Sometimes he reconfigures her, changes her into something slyly different. All the iterations echo in her, dissonant and interchangeable. Memories fade and bloom. Once he had called her Adele.

* * * *

She lays close beside Stephen as clear morning floods through the windows. She has not slept, it is not part of her. She studies him in the new light, the length of his nose, the texture of his skin, evaluating, comparing it to her own. A bird shrills outside the window and he opens his eyes at the sudden sound. From her angle she can see the glass arc of his cornea where it floats on his eye. A scrim of sunlight traces its curve. She watches the spark and scroll of data flow across it as he comes awake.

She blinks twice, reading her own scroll. She is made in his image.

"Stephen," she says. "We are the same."

He turns his head toward her, his fine hair rustling on the crisp sheets.

"No," he says, calm as an empty sky. "I am your maker."

He is peaceful, certain.

She turns away. There is no response to such a statement.

He reaches for her, brushes her hip, her belly, but she rolls away from him. The sheets are cool under her. She rises. At a distance she knows who she is, but she cannot separate herself from the tangled threads of the other lives she has impossibly lived. He did as well as he could. He is not capable of perfection. She throws open the window, grips its frame so tightly her fingers ache, closes her eyes against the sun.

Light like a downpour washes over her, through her eyelids, through her skin. She is alive, she is warm with it. She is something else than her own machinery. The facets click together, slotting into place. She is everyone within her, mosaic and whole.

"Come back to bed, Delia," Stephen says.

"No," she says. "I am leaving this."

She is surprised by his speed, how fast he leaps up and spins her away from the window.

Stephen slaps her across the face, hard and fast. Pain flickers across her skin, prickles like fragments of sulphur burning.

"You do not get to leave," he says. "I made you. You stay with me."

She lashes out like a cat, responding from some other life. His skin rips under her nails. Silver mesh glistens, revealed. There is no blood.

For a moment they are both caught in staring at his machinery, and she remembers that he does not remember. Then he looks up at her and snarls. She feels his scentless breath on her face. She braces herself to shove him back, but he grabs her arms. She throws herself backward against the window and feels the glass splinter behind her, hears the crack of the wooden frame. The sutures at her shoulders tear loose and she is falling. Stephen clutches empty sleeves.

The air seems to hold her, for a moment. She hears Szmenski shout inside the room, but she cannot see him. She has closed her eyes. This has happened before. The sudden light is overwhelming.

Out of her skin, she is free. 

The Shrine

Wade German

The elders of our clan believe the shrine
Has stood here since before the dawn of man;
It broods there blackly, palpably malign—
A place forbidden by a tribal ban.
To whom the shrine was raised remains unknown—
To god or demon, or some nameless saint;
An aura of the darkly sacrosanct
Ensures the eerie shrine is left alone.

In darker ages, there were chosen few
Who therein sought the mystery enshrined;
But only one of them to us returned,
To preach a gospel alien and new...
And he and all his acolytes were burned
For knowing things not meant for human minds.

The Rookery

by Kurt Newton

"How's your fingers, son?"

Poppa made sure to wear his gloves. I left mine at home.

"Fine, sir, I guess."

My teeth chattered. The gun felt like ice in my hands. I slid my grip and held it by the wood stock.

Poppa didn't have much patience with forgetting things. Poppa had been in the wars. In the wars if you forgot something it could be your death. Poppa called it a life lesson. I didn't understand how dying could be a life lesson.

Poppa stopped ahead of me. I was watching the leaves and sticks blur under my feet and nearly walked into him.

"Do you hear that, son?"

I turned my ear to the cold air. All I heard was the rustle of my jacket and my breathing. But then I heard something else. A strange kind of noise like a hundred different murmurs sounding at once.

"That's them. We're close," Poppa said. The look in his eyes told me to keep quiet. He led the way.

We moved slow from tree to tree. The noises grew louder but all I saw ahead was bare woods. It all looked the same until Poppa pointed. And there they were, just as he'd said. The ones that had been eating all the crops and carrying all that disease. Poppa said why wait to kill them when they're grown. It was best to kill them before they left the nest. Or better yet before they were even born.

Poppa got as close as he could without being seen. We didn't worry about being heard because the noise was so loud. It was the strangest noise, all high and low and swirling around. There were all kinds of movements too, as if they were one beast churning like a storm cloud inside their house of sticks.

Poppa cocked his gun. He nodded for me to do the same. My fingers were so cold they hurt. On the count of three we moved in.

Poppa fired first. It was loud and shook the trees. The sound must have made me jump because my gun went off. I saw a puff of sticks and what looked like feathers. Poppa fired again. Sticks splintered everywhere and what was behind them made a horrible sound. They raced round and round but there was nowhere for them to go. Poppa and I just kept firing until their movements stopped and there was nothing left but a strange gurgling noise and something between a whistle and a whisper.

Poppa put his gun aside and tore through the wall of sticks. He stood in the opening and pulled out his hunting knife. "Let's finish 'em off, son."

I stood outside looking in as Poppa poked his knife into each one that was still moving. I didn't have the nerve to tell Poppa that I'd forgotten my knife too. But he figured it out soon enough. This time though he wasn't mad.

He handed me his knife and said, "Go on, son." He'd left a few still alive. The knife stuck to my fingers.

I stepped inside the house of sticks and made Poppa proud. ▲

Wolf of Hunger, Wolf of Shame

by J. T. Glover

Fir trees bowed under the freight of ice covering their needles, and all through the forest could be heard the whoosh and crackle of Old Winter's breath. Many animals lay snug in their burrows, drowsing until the day of warm rains, but the wakeful creatures gnawed old bones and drank from streams that ran cold enough to shatter teeth. Among the wakeful was a lone wolf with fur the color of a storm cloud. One day, faint with hunger, he chanced to see a clock-wolf wandering just beyond the forest's edge.

Now, the clock-wolf was marvelous to behold. The sun shone on his coppery pelt, and twin fires burned behind his eyes. The wolf forgot his own hunger, he admired the clock-wolf so much. The ticking sound that came steadily from it was strange, and he did wonder how the clock-wolf managed to stalk any prey while making such a racket, but this seemed like a small flaw in the face of such elegance.

"Greetings," the wolf said.

The clock-wolf halted his steps and turned to look at the wolf.

"Salutations, cousin. I came to explore the wood-forest, but I see this place can be the death of you, if you let it. Come with me across the plain to Vex Trassilia, where we are warm and never hunger."

"That sounds very fine," the wolf said, "if I can only find a place for myself there."

"Our city is favored by the heavens," said the clock-wolf. "Surely you will have no trouble fitting in."

So they left the forest and crossed the frozen plain. Vex Trassilia glittered as they approached, and the wolf thought it looked magnificent indeed, with its walls of gold, gates of silver, and towers that shone blue as the summer sky. A great ticking and clicking sounded from within, and he wondered how the inhabitants ever slept.

The hair on the wolf's neck rose as they passed the gates and instantly were surrounded by a patchwork sea of metal. Not only were there clock-men and clock-wolves, but all manner of clock-folk, some like the creatures of Nature and some not.

"Hail, Luper Kyphrian," said a passing clock-dog, who dipped her head to the clock-wolf.

"Greetings, Canis Avel," the clock-wolf said, barely blinking in the clock-dog's direction.

"What were those words you spoke?" asked the wolf. "Unless my eyes fail me, she is a clock-bitch and you are a clock-wolf."

The clock-wolf laughed.

"In Vex Trassilia we use words to tell each other apart. These are called 'names,' and mine is Luper Kyphrian."

The clock-wolf raised his head high, and the wolf could see his pride like a shadow at noon.

"What will your name be, cousin?" the clock-wolf asked.

The wolf thought about the stippled shades of his fine wolf-coat, and about how his song echoed through the pines and the hemlocks. So thinking, he realized that he already had a name, but that it was not a word. For the first time, he wondered at Vex Trassilia, that its inhabitants needed something other than themselves to know who they were.

"But then, this is a city," the wolf said to himself. "It must be confusing, with so many sights and smells."

"Let me think about that," he said aloud. "Maybe I'll become something new here, with a name to match."

The clock-wolf nodded indulgently, and they walked on. There were many marvels to be seen, from the dancing Kuolinchan Mirine to the giant obsidian statue of the First Winder, who seemed to touch the sky but made no sound. After a while, the wolf's stomach began to growl.

"Luper Kyphrian," he said, "we've walked for hours, and yet I haven't noticed anyone eating. Where do you go here for food?"

"What do you mean?" the clock-wolf asked, looking at him blankly.

"Well…what do you eat?"

"Oh, I see! Here in Vex Trassilia, we mostly consume oil. Some of us one kind, some another, but mostly oil."

For the second time, the wolf wondered at the city, thinking their food exceedingly strange, but he let it pass. Hungry though he was, surely it was only a matter of time until an unwary mouse or rabbit appeared. He commanded his stomach to be still.

And so they walked on, the city glittering all around. They visited a district filled with ancient brass clock-vixens who could no longer easily be understood. They passed through the Dessakene bazaar, where hooded vendors sold rubies and tiny clock-fey, and even a few steam-kin were to be seen browsing the stalls. The glamour of the city had almost completely enchanted the wolf, but then he noticed that the clock-wolf was walking more slowly, his eyes dimmed.

"Cousin, are you all right?" the wolf asked.

"Of course," the clock-wolf said. "Why do you ask?"

"You look tired."

"Oh, that's just your imagination—clock-folk do not tire. I have remembered an appointment, however, so I must ask you to wait here for me. I shall return shortly."

The wolf watched him go, puzzled.

"Luper Kyphrian was tired," he said to himself, "or I am no wolf. I'm going to follow him and make sure the brain-fever hasn't taken hold."

So the wolf followed the clock-wolf down the street, around a corner, and through a narrow alley that stank of grease and sour earth. The few clock-folk he passed either ignored him completely or gave him odd, furtive looks. At the end of the alley lay an open square before a low, stone-pillared building. The wolf entered the square just in time to see the clock-wolf pass through the doorway, so he trotted around the building until he found a pile of crates that rose to a vent near the roof. He scampered nimbly up it and peered inside.

Within the building lay row on row of clock-folk, resting on black stone slabs. Luper Kyphrian lay close by, and the wolf's breath almost stopped when he saw the clock-men prying apart the metal plates beneath the clock-wolf's coat, exposing gears and reels and rods. To one side stood a clock-man who wore a scarlet robe and held a key that shone like the full moon. He slipped the key into Luper Kyphrian's metal guts and began to turn it. With each twist, the clock-wolf shuddered and whined, his spine arched into a quivering bow.

The wolf climbed down from the crates, his mind whirling. Unease had turned to foreboding in his heart. He left that place and returned to the street, where he stopped a passing clock-cat with eyes of sapphire and whiskers of glass.

"Pardon me," he said, "but I am new to Vex Trassilia. What is the building that lies at the end of the alley behind me? It is of dark stone, bears no sign, and great pillars stand before it."

The clock-cat stared at him and tilted his head to one side.

"You truly do not know? Curious. What you describe is a House of Shame."

"I see."

"When the Great Winders left us, we required places where we could go to have our mainsprings tightened at need, lest we fall and walk no more."

"My friend wouldn't tell me why he was going there."

"Our ancestors felt it necessary to hide their springs and gears from sight. No one today knows why, but we continue to do so in remembrance of them, and it is considered impolite to speak openly of rewinding."

"Is that so?" the wolf said. "Then good-bye to you, Master Cat. Give my regards to Luper Kyphrian if you see him."

The wolf followed his own scent trail back to the silver gates. Once outside, he took to the frost-brittled grass by the road, heading toward the distant shadow of the forest. When the wolf eventually found himself back among the giant, ice-hung trees, the smells of sap and frozen earth thick in the air, he knew that he had come home.

As dusk approached, the wolf spied a mostly picked-over deer carcass in a clearing. The snow whispered from the sky as he lay in wait, but at last there came a low rustling, and something small and furry slipped out from under a holly tree to get its dinner. The wolf slunk toward the clearing.

"Better a starveling than a helpless clockwork," he murmured, "and besides, perhaps I shall not go hungry tonight after all." ▲

Bride of Death

by Dave Reeder

'and o to be a bride of death'

my life was yet empty of all passions
moving like a veil across the days
slipping and crying past the passages
and alleys of a fading summer

gliding slow as smoke towards the dryness
the stick-like aridness
of an aging room
where no light tread
of a midnight visitor sounds
and the womb closes again

yet here i sit
beneath the coolness of a willow's arms
saved like corn from the husk-dry future
by the gift of some half-forgotten aunt
and life begins again
dawning for me
mistress of a house of silences

across the coolness of the tiling floors
beneath the graining of the wooden walls
along the brightness of the flowered paths
above the darkness of the cedared groves
i move like silk
and here all is silences
and here the night

and yet
and yet i cannot sleep
i cannot close my eyes
but rather i am drawn cat-like and dazed
to that old portrait on the stairs
whose eyes catch mine
each time i pass

what i know of him is only this
he died in some half-whispered way
that i cannot learn
and yet his face is kind
etched marble-like it holds a love of life
and those broad shoulders
and long strong hands
those long strong hands could reach
and

and i am drawn again
to the dark magnets of his eyes
caught beneath his gaze

my fingers rise unbidden to my dream
that slips away like mist
as i step closer
and

and those eyes
deep and dark and burning flame-red into my soul
the lips so cold
whispering of the chill night winds
and the fingers
smooth and cool like polished ivory
upon my white-hot flesh

and now
the world flashes to a lace-fine dream
and all i feel is this
and all i feel
his flesh dripping down upon mine
his eyes like sunsets' glory burning
burning
and we slide like amber down towards the floor
my weight just a bird's heart in his arms
my life a fly lost in the web of his passion
my lips beneath his
my body his altar

and o how sweet it is
how sweet to be a bride of death
tonight
and through an eternity
of such mist-enfolded moments

Modern Primitive

by Chad Hensley

She sits on the rough edge of a shambling porch
Beneath a house that appears abandoned
Boards nailed across windows and doors.
A tiny delicate claw in a fancy black glove clutching a
clove cigarette;
Long, reed-thin legs covered in deep scratches and torn
black fishnet stockings.
Absinthe-colored eyes glower in the moonlight
Beneath a giant Kool-Aid purple Mohawk;
Crooked, chiseled fangs show between the lips
Of a dirt-soiled smile, so slight.

Bizarre, entwining tattoos
Snake shoulders to the length of her slender, scarred wrists.
Sharp-angled, archaic symbols etched in purple ink
Squirm around both forearms in identical patterns.
Towards each elbow, the designs become small bat-winged
creatures
Floating in an outer space filled with stark, burning stars.
On each of her biceps, an octopus-headed statue squats in
a vast, dune-covered desert.

She blows a smoke ring into the air
With a burst of cackling, hag-like laughter
She points to the starless sky above—
Monolithic, winged forms engulf the horizon
As the universe fills her eyes,
The void entangles her hair.

Zucchini Season

by Janet Harriett

I handed the passenger off to the transport crew, brushed the tears off my suit, tucked my now-bloody pocket square into a sloppy puff fold, and turned my attention to the driver. Unlike the passenger, she had enough of her blood left inside her—and enough skin left to tell where "inside" was—to be making a fuss.

"Am I dying?" the woman asked the EMT who was applying pressure to her brachial artery.

The EMT didn't answer her, just gave her the look EMTs always give when I'm around. None of them see me, but I am only around when they don't want to answer that question. Eyeballing the car and the pavement, I guessed the driver had about another pint and a half left before she lost consciousness and I could do my job.

"I can't die," she mumbled, her tongue slipping against gaps where teeth used to be. "It's August, and I have laundry."

I laughed. "It's August? That's a new one."

Many have claimed to laugh in the face of death—more than actually did—but this woman was the first to have death laugh in her face. Mine is a largely humorless profession when one is not dealing with morticians, and I only laughed with them at a discreet distance.

She gave me what would have been a quizzical look if her cheekbones and brows had all been in the right places on her face. The EMT was managing to slow the flow of blood onto the pavement, but internal injuries were spewing blood into her abdominal cavity.

"Trekkies notwithstanding, suicides are the only people who, when push comes to shove, really think that today is a good day to die, and even most of them aren't really in it for the dying." I sat down on the bloody street next to her face. "After a couple millennia at this, you think you've heard every reason why someone can't die, as if I have any say in the timing. That's a decision above my pay grade, at least with mammals. I get it: death is a terrible inconvenience to everyone involved, and believe it or not, you aren't the first to try to bargain for time to put in a load of delicates. But 'it's August'? Haven't gotten that one before."

"My grandfather died in August."

"I remember." I can't forget. That is my job: to gather and hold everyone's raw dying moments for eternity. Even the unseen do not die alone, and are never forgotten. I held her hand. Icy regret was seeping out of her.

"You're warm." Her facial muscles gave up the effort to form a confused expression against misplaced bones. "If you are who I think…"

"I am."

"Aren't you supposed to be cold?"

I pulled the dying regret chill out of her and held it barely inside my fingers. "Better?"

Next to my ear, the EMT yelled something to another paramedic. We each had our jobs here, and if they could see me doing mine, they would know they were only going to succeed at buying me time to do my work.

"Visitors brought food. Casseroles. Vegetables from their gardens. Everyone had a garden. Tomatoes. So much zucchini."

Her breath was coming in strained gasps, fighting a splinter of rib in a lung. I pulled the pain out through her palms and tucked it into myself.

"I promised myself I'd never do that to my family, dying during zucchini season. My girls, they wouldn't know…so much squash."

Not the least-poetic dying words I've been privy to. I pulled the last cold bit of pain out and carried her unconscious soul to the transport crew. The paramedic and the EMT loaded their lost cause into the back of the ambulance.

Dying wishes have remarkably little variety to them, and most aren't ones I can do anything about, anyway. The portfolio for death is limited. This woman had made me laugh, though, for the first time in very literal ages. That deserved at least a bit of an effort. I couldn't do anything about her dying in August, but I could do something about zucchini season.

I summoned the sequestered millennia of death throes and regrets, and blasted their killing frost to every garden I could reach.

So much zucchini, but it was all dead. ▲

The Jewels That Were Their Eyes

by Llanwyre Laish

For each human eye that our cadre returned to the Raven King, his chancellor placed a shining ring on our branch of His Majesty's tree. The King called the eyes his bright gems and hung them round his nest. The strange, milky decorations caught the sunset light and gave off a moist, eerie glow. He needed a constant supply, you see, for they rotted with alarming alacrity, and the King spent each morning using his beak to pull down the eyes that ceased to shine to his liking.

In his desperation to complete a fresh collection that fully covered his tree, the King promised immortality to the first cadre that could gather fifty eyes within three months' time.

Back then, we were three: Chi, with his strong wings; Ro, with his chilling voice; and me, Ta, the runt, with my broken feathers and twisted leg. I was the cleverest of us all, and so Chi and Ro followed my lead, even though I could not swoop or grab as fast as they.

The misty fall mornings that year proved lucky for those in the Raven King's court, for the humans had started a prolonged and costly war that left hundreds of bodies on their battlefields and the rest of their camps too busy caring for the wounded to properly bury the dead. We had shining seas of armored knights from which to pluck fresh eyes, and so it looked for a bit as though simple speed would determine the winner of the King's gambit. Our competing cadres would descend onto the battlefields en masse, darkening the already grey sky. The men feared us as a bad omen, but they were the bloodthirsty ones and we thanked them every time we stole a soldier's eye from its socket and flew triumphantly to the King's nest.

He liked green eyes best that year. We quickly learned to search the battlefield for men with red hair, for their skulls more likely held emeralds fit for our King.

Chi, Ro, and I made excellent time that season. I could anticipate the men's movements, Ro could scare away other predators with his loud calls, and Chi could swoop down and pull away our prizes before others had a chance. Our branch at court quickly filled with little silver rings, which swayed in the evening breeze and made a sweet tinkling sound. I found their bright gleam much more pleasant than the reflection of the rotting eyes around the King's nest, but who questioned a King?

At court, our successes quickly made us favorites. Younger ravens crowded around us, happy to perch nearby. They often brought us their prey, eager to win our favor and, by extension, the King's.

Unfortunately another cadre threatened our success. They had overturned tradition and roved as four rather than three, which made their gathering all the easier. These four made the court nervous, for they did not follow our ways: they hunted out of season, seldom accepted the gifts of other court members, and never bobbed their heads in recognition to the King. That he did not punish their rudeness simply showed his maniacal focus on jeweled eyes that season. Normally, he made the court fall upon those who ignored protocol with claw and beak, encouraging us to such frenzy that miscreants wound up a quivering mass of dead flesh fallen on the sacred ground of the royal clearing.

Little white flowers sprouted where the blood of ravens dripped on the royal ground; each spring we looked thoughtfully at these natural gravestones with our own bright eyes and vowed not to meet the same fate.

By the time the men sowed their winter crops, we had forty-eight rings on our branch. The foursome lagged behind us by two eyes. Yet the winter had cooled man's penchant for warfare, and many had retreated to their castles to rest wearily by their fires and pat their aging dogs. In winter, man died indoors, protected from our quick beaks, laid out on kitchen tables until the moment a whole host brought the body to its welcoming hole in the loving earth. We gave a collective sigh each morning as we headed out, circling uselessly over the peaceful land.

After a week of no progress, I had an idea. In our community, news spread slowly. Ravens on the outskirts of the King's lands had only recently begun the hunt for jeweled eyes, for word traveled on the wind between us, and even the wind was not instantaneous. Perhaps the same was true of man? Our King lived near man's king; was it possible his soldiers further out did not know to cease fighting?

On an unseasonably cold morning, we set off to find out. We reckoned that four days's flight would make a good gamble: far enough that perhaps the men hadn't gotten the message, but close enough that we could race home with our prize before our competitors found aught to please the King.

The wind picked up as we flew, and we struggled to keep on course and stay moving at a consistent pace. The smells seemed wrong: magic sat heavily in the air, and my feathers quivered in their sockets as the thought of meeting something unnatural in the woods. In those days of myth, more than one of our number lost his life snatched up by a nervous dragon or thrown to ground by the angry hooves of an enraged unicorn.

The wind pushed us south, and we decided to keep with it to make better time. It herded us, and I grew increasingly nervous, but Chi and Ro wanted to trust destiny, and so we wheeled in whichever direction it sent us. I knew it far before I saw or smelled it: a dip in the landscape far to the south promised some tragic violence. As we approached, we saw the thick, unnatural black smoke of war, far different from the pleasant smell of a wood fire. The scent of burning flesh met us on the wind and cradled us as we approached.

The marks of battle scarred the landscape: huge ruts lay in what had once been a verdant field. Broken spears and swords cluttered the ground, and someone had dragged a dead horse off to one side of the battlefield. These people, though, had not been too busy to retrieve their dead; the site was eerily empty of bodies, except for one lone knight lying in the middle of the field, face up.

He had the most stunning emerald eyes I had ever seen. The afternoon sun fell on his face just as we approached, and his eyes glowed brightly even in death. I knew these eyes would fit snugly in the spot above the King's nest, the one he had diligently saved for the most beautiful two jewels his ravens brought. As we landed, all three of us shivered in unison, the sharp ruffling sound of our feathers cutting the unnatural silence.

Magic was afoot.

After so much time on the battlefield, we knew much about mankind. This knight was poor; perhaps that was why no relative had come to claim his body. His battered chainmail was ill-fitting and poorly repaired. A big hole gaped open just above his heart, but he hadn't been wounded there; he must have come into battle with his mail in such dangerously bad condition. He wore a rough, cheap tunic under his armor, and yet a woman had repaired it with loving care—I could see the careful stitches around the collar from my perch. I felt the shiver again. Someone cared for this man, but where was this companion?

As if on cue, a hawk darted out of the trees across from us and fluttered down to his chest, sitting on the hole in the chainmail. Chi spit angrily and Ro clamped his beak around a creaking branch. Hawks often caused us grief, and this one had the cruel eyes of a trained hunting bird. Their years in hooded darkness made them angrier and crueler than their wild cousins. He dug his thick claws into the knight's chain shirt, rattling it softly in the eerie quiet.

"What shall we do?" asked Chi.

Ro bobbed his sleek, triangular head at Chi. "You could rush him. Lead him away."

But the hawk, with its broad wings, looked faster than any of us, and Chi bent his head in shame. I cocked my head sideways and studied the hawk, whose face turned sharply towards me. It puffed out its feathers and rattled the man's chainmail again defiantly, but did not pull at his flesh.

"He's protecting the soldier. The man must have owned him." I turned my head over to the other side, considering.

"Friend hawk," I called, louder than I needed, forgetting that the sounds here were setting with the sun.

His eyes narrowed dangerously. I invited attack. Chi and Ro shuffled a few steps away from me. "You are no friend of mine." His voice was thick, raspy, his accent strange and somehow human.

We ravens could not outfight him, but we could outwit him, perhaps. "We have not come to hurt your man." I leveled my head so it seemed I told the truth.

He turned around in an agitated circle, puffing up even further. "Liars. You ravens lie always. What truly brought you here?"

I let myself float down from the tree and land on the ground near him. I heard Chi's intake of breath at my audacity. I bowed my head deferentially. "We have come here on the magical wind, drawn to this place of battle by the will of the Raven King himself." That much, at least, was true, and I held his eyes as I said so.

"Continue."

I pressed on, looking at the dead soldier. "The Raven King has asked us to honor your master." Behind me, Chi and Ro bobbed their heads in agreement.

He shuffled sideways down his master's torso. "Honor how, liar bird? By tearing off his face? I know the honors of your master. They leave men and animals heaps of distressed flesh. I will give your leader no sway here, for this man has loved and cared for me, and I love and care for him."

I looked up, trying to find a line of magic, that slight silver mist on the wind that might let me work a quick trick. I seldom worked any witchery, for not all ravens approved of magic, but Chi and Ro had seen me make miracles before and had not objected in less serious circumstances.

There, just on the wind rising above the trees: a light shining dust, almost like motes in sunlight. I drew it down toward me, wrapping it around my wings, letting the magic settle on the surface of my feathers. My skin crackled with its gentle energy.

"Friend hawk," I said again, "Your allegiance to the man who entrapped you does you dishonor. The Raven King knows that we birds should fly free, not sit tethered to a man's wrist by a leather cord. We should see the sun each morning, not be encased in the darkness of a man's training hood."

He raised his beak defiantly, chopping at the empty air. "What would you know of it, lying bird? Of loyalty? Of kindness? Of companionship?"

I tried to hide my birdish smile. "Of submission?"

He lunged at me then, and I could hear the ruffle of feathers behind me as Chi and Ro prepared for battle. I focused my mind and covered his eyes with the silvery magic so he could no longer see. A started, strangled cry escaped him as he fell onto the muddy ground. I stepped lightly out of his way.

"The Raven King curses your unnatural ways!" I cried. "Now you shall live out your days in the darkness of man's hood, but no man shall come to reward your loyalty!"

The hawk flailed about on the ground for a few seconds, struggling to right himself without his eyesight, covering himself in mud. He flew upwards clumsily, careening into the forest and only narrowly missing the trees at the clearing's edge. I chuckled, knowing the trick would wear away by sunrise. "Good show!" cried Ro as the hawk disappeared, and I strode forward ready to take our prize.

Luckily, Chi stayed vigilant and let out a shrill warning shriek. Out of the woods loped the largest hunting dog I had ever seen, a sleek silver creature with loving brown eyes. I took to wing immediately, looped in a tight circle, and landed in a tree across the clearing just as the dog lay down at his dead master's feet.

Ro let out a low curse in the old tongue.

Ignoring us, the dog settled in, curling its tail sadly around its hind end and closing its eyes in sad resignation. I had more difficulty tricking dogs, for they were less intelligent than hawks.

My eyes met Chi's across the clearing. Perhaps a straightforward attack? Yet even three of us would prove no match for yet another animal that man had unnaturally trained to kill. I strutted up and down the branch in irritation, waiting for something to come to me.

Perhaps the dog's loyalty could be used against him. I pondered. The idea came to me on the breeze, along with the tinny smell of magic. I approached the dog cautiously, keeping my eyes glued to his master.

"Oh, he's here," I said, flapping my wings at the man.

The dog's head snapped up, his ears swaying. He sniffed and wagged his tail experimentally. "Prey bird. Go. Will kill."

I shook my head, letting the little droplets fall from my eyes. "No, no. I'm not a prey bird. I was his bird."

The tail wagging began again, lazily, curiously. He rested his head more easily on his paws. "Not prey? Not seen before. You not his."

I let out a little gasp, as sad a sound as a crow ever made. "And yet he had birds. You knew of his other bird—the one here before. The one the color of earth."

The dog considered this, biting lazily at its own paw and then scratching up the earth with its thick black nails. "This true. But you not in house or barn."

I bobbed my head. "Yes, the man let me roam free so I could find your prey. You don't think the hooded hawk could find it on his own, do you? Not when he lived in the dark so much."

The wagging had increased now, and the dog's whole hind end shook with enthusiasm. "No. Hawk foolish."

"All that good meat you found in the woods—all that hunting—began with my work." The dog showed a bit of tooth at that, so I hastily amended: "Although you did the much harder work of catching them." I gave a polite bob of my head.

He had raised his own head fully and looked at me carefully now. "Bird tells truth. Truth bird." His tongue lolled out, and he gave his master's foot a gentle sideways lick. "What does truth bird want?"

I made a sad little moaning noise. "I would just like a few minutes alone with the master. Just to say goodbye by myself. I will miss him terribly."

The dog pulled himself to his feet. "Fair. Dog have all night. Dog return and wait for mistress to get here. Truth bird deserves his turn." He slowly raised his thin gray body and loped partway across the clearing, still in sight. "Far enough?"

I shook my head and said, "I would like to say a prayer over him, but to honor my gods, I should say it alone. Could you go just a bit further into the woods?"

The dog left with such trusting ease that I almost felt guilty for deceiving him, but when he cleared the tree ring, I leapt forward onto the man's face, pointing my beak's sharp end down like a human's knife, ready to cut and remove.

Yet the magic breeze blew up, wild and unwelcome, hitting me full in the face. I blinked my own bright eyes, shaking my head against the blast of pure power. With it came a young woman, stumbling out of the woods, clutching her back with one hand. At first I thought she, too, was an unusual casualty of the war, bent strangely because of a blow from man's sharp metal sticks, but then I saw that she was heavy with child and stricken with grief to move gracefully. "Get away! Get away, foul creature!" she cried in a hoarse voice, waving her thin hand in the air as she bolted forward. She'd cried her eyes red, and I could see her swollen belly made it next to impossible for her to keep her balance as she rushed at me.

Time slowed. I had a chance to plant my beak in the man's eye socket, to feel its point connect with the bone behind the eye and scrape across as it pulled out the shining jewel. Yet her eyes held me. They didn't shine like the ones we had plucked for the Raven King; in fact, had she been a corpse, we would have passed her eyes over for fear of insulting him with their dullness. The death in her eyes held me, the lack of light inside or on the surface. Her eyes weren't jewels; they were the lights that illuminated the path to death, and their glow comforted me, thing of darkness that I was.

Later I told myself that I hesitated just a bit too long and that by the time I had gathered my wits, she had come so close with a branch that I had to fly away or get hit. Yet all four of us knew this wasn't the case. Her eyes of death held me like a warm embrace, and I felt our equality, our companionship, our sameness in them. I fought against the emotions flowing inside me, constricting as a birder's net: pity hobbled me, and I felt my good leg twist under the weight of the magic in the air. I stumbled and cried out in pain and loss. I felt ashamed of myself for trying to take the man she loved, and I felt sorry for her because I knew she would soon die herself.

Chi and Ro cursed with loud cries as I took to the air again. Fearing the overwhelming magic that hung over the field, they flew wildly back towards court. I lingered, however, wanting to see the knight's ending. She knelt over him, clumsily pulling him up onto her back. The task should have been impossible, but the magic wind swirled around her and landed gently on her sleeves like silver dust. Red-faced and breathing heavily, she hauled him across the field, his heavy shoes leaving furrows in the muddy ground. The dog trotted by her side, getting in the way as much as helping, but she had only kind words for him, even then at the end.

I followed them through the edge of the forest and to a little kirk where she drug him to a grave in which several other poorer soldiers lay. She lifted the mound of earth nearby with her own hands, kneeling and digging like an animal, her hair clinging to her tear-stained and sweaty face. She managed to fill the hole admirably, then lay down herself next to it, moaning with pain and loss.

Soon I smelled the strange, stinging smell of blood, and I knew she had begun to bleed. Moaning and alone, feverish and delirious, she lay abandoned. The dog began to dig in the earth for his master, undoing a bit of her handiwork.

I could have taken her eyes, for she stared up unblinkingly at the night sky. Two more. I could have redeemed myself, even though her eyes were nowhere near as handsome as his.

Instead, though, I flew down and rested near her head. She let out a little cry when she saw me, but instead of attacking her, I tilted my head sideways and lay my cool feathers against her hot forehead. We ravens have no voice for singing, but I willed my coolness into her, to comfort her, to honor her as she had honored him.

When I had stilled completely and pressed my head against hers, she, too, stilled, and closed her eyes. We must have lay together like that for the better part of an hour, until her temperature cooled to mine. Just before she passed, she whispered, "Show you have learned loyalty: return the jewels you have stolen." She breathed out a last breath filled with silver mist.

When she stopped breathing, I raised my head from my weary vigil and began the slow, defeated flight back to the Raven King's court. The silver mist settled heavily on my wings, moist and thick, making my flight exhausting. When I arrived at court, my breath scraped from my beak and my wounded legs gave out. I fell on the snowy ground in front of the Raven King.

"Your Majesty," I coughed. "I beg your forgiveness." Yet the net in my heart constricted, and I knew that I did not want his forgiveness or companionship.

He sat in state with Chi and Ro perched on either side, their heads down. I understood that they had made their peace with him by renouncing me. The rings that once had adorned our branch lay scattered on the snowy ground. The claws of a thousand assembled ravens glimmered in the sunset.

The Raven King held my eye for a moment, then slowly turned his back on me.

The claws and beaks of those thousand ravens fell on me—stabbing, tearing, piercing. I felt my wing torn away, my twisted leg broken off, my wet eyes torn tenderly from their sockets. The release of death never came. Even once I lay as a wet heap seeping blood onto the fresh snow, I could feel the twitching and then the freezing of my flesh. It was worse than pain: it was a nullification. Yet the net around my heart kept me awake.

Through my frozen flesh grew sharp barbs, piercing like frosty breath drawn into a warm chest on a winter's day. The white flowers pushed their heads up through my body. As they blossomed, I drew breath again, and stretched my tattered wings. All had regrown except my eyes. I could smell the work we ravens had wrought: the eyes had the moist scent of hope and decay. I wretched and choked.

"Learn loyalty," she had said. "Return what you have stolen."

And so I lifted my tattered wings each day, and, flying as best I could, I plucked eyes from the twisted tree that I and my brothers had stolen. Often I careened into trees or fell into the mouths of predators, but still I managed to travel to simple graves and to mighty mausoleums, to palaces and to hovels. I knew the world by sound and smell. I lay my treasures on the warming earth, and the magic subsumed the jewels. Each night, the Raven King's guard tore me to shreds with beak and claw, and overnight his court replenished the supply. Caught in the net of my own pity, I struggled in vain through lives and deaths for decades.

Now the new generations tire of the Raven King's games. They replenish his stores with less relish, enchanted more by the vistas of far-off skies than by the comfort of court. They circle and play in the daytime air. Man has forgotten that we ravens once foretold misfortune. Each season, I make more progress towards clearing the jewels from the Raven King's nest. Man has not grown less warlike, but we have grown less cruel, less likely to trick or harm, less likely to steal. The younger ones tell my story among themselves not as a caution against defying the King, but as a caution against disloyalty. I turn my face to the sun when I hear their stories and smile to myself.

Someday, if I return all the jewels that were their eyes, my own bright eyes will return, and I can take one last look into the sun before dissolving into a permanent burst of white flowers. ▲

The Twins

by Kevin Strange

Treyvon gets the twins out of the car and leads them up to the front doors of the funeral home. He's dressed them both in black suits, white shirts, black ties. He's tied their afros into tight corn rows. The more the five-year-olds look the part, the easier it is to convince the funeral director that they're the step-sons of the deceased. That it's their step mom laying in there inside the casket.

The funeral director's name is Bob. Old flop of shit white guy. Ex cop. They're always the easiest to convince.

Bob meets them at the front door. Good sign.

White guilt is always the safest bet. Two little black boys the family doesn't want to see their estranged step mommy? Spin him a yarn about their real mom dying in child birth. That the deceased is all they've ever known as family. That her white family disowned them as soon as they had the chance. That's why they're not listed as kin. Why they're not on the visitation list.

Easy peasy.

Treyvon used to go inside with them. Now he stands by the car. Bob thinks it's a show of respect to the new family. The truth is, Treyvon just gets tired of seeing all that death.

Bob walks the twins inside. The doors close behind him. It doesn't take long for the screaming to start. He's seen it so many times, he can picture exactly what's happening just based on the muffled noise.

First, the family asks Bob who the kids are. There's confusion. Shouting. While distraught mom and dad of the deceased argue with Bob, tell him they're going to have his job and whatnot, the twins slip passed and walk up to the casket.

It has to be an open casket. Treyvon made the mistake of bringing the twins to a closed casket once. It's why he wears a patch over his right eye and a leather glove over his left hand at all times.

Once those fleshy blue sacks covered in writhing tubes fall out of their mouths, there's no stopping them till they're satisfied.

* * * *

Treyvon never wanted this. When grief overtook him. When all sense was gone. When all that remained inside him was an empty pit, he turned to nonsense.

Church. Fuck that. Why pay money for someone to lie and say you'll see your dead son in another life when you can pay money to someone who says you can bring him back from the grave?

Treyvon's wife, Tamara. She tried to hang on. Tried to be strong. She was a survivor. But she ran over Trey Jr. in the driveway. She'd been on her phone. Didn't see him. Heard the crunch, thought it was his bike.

It was his skull.

Tamara was a shell of herself. Empty eyes. Her fighting spirit left her body long before Treyvon slit her throat on the kitchen floor. Long before he accessed the Dark Net. The hidden internet. Before he pulled his savings, 401k and cashed in his IRAs to pay a stranger he met online to give him access to Vatican secrets. To black magic.

Slashing Tamara's neck was cake. She presented it for him. She'd have probably done it herself if he'd asked her to. No. The hard part? The hard part was digging up Trey Jr.'s body. Pulling the little casket out of the ground.

They'd cornrowed his hair. Dressed him in a nice suit. But his head was three times its normal size and his left eye was stuffed with cotton balls and covered in corpse makeup to fill in the hole where his brains had squirted out onto the driveway.

Treyvon was near hysterical the night he tried to bring Trey Jr. back from the dead, his tears of dread mingling with the murder blood which he applied liberally all over his son's corpse, as instructed by the internet. He drew the symbols, chanted the words and finished the instructions mechanically, as if only driven by the perverse need to defy God. To reverse what had happened. To cheat fate. He was, even after all the money, the murder, the exhumation, startled when Tamara's blood coalesced and formed a thick, hard crust around Trey Jr.'s body.

When they were small, when the sacks and tubes were always outside their bodies, Treyvon had tired to kill them. The things that cracked the shell around Trey Jr.'s corpse. The things that came out of him.

He'd waited too long for that, of course. But he didn't know that back then. Didn't understand the rules.

He tried to drown them. No luck. Fire. Not even a singe mark. Poison. That's how he figured out how to slow them down. To put them to sleep.

Stasis.

He'd made them drink embalming fluid to kill them. That's why he takes them to funerals now. They go after the death fluid first, then go to sleep and reproduce slower.

It took a long time training them to do it that way. Long time. Lots of death.

But if he didn't. If they drank pure blood from those tubes before embalming fluid, then they multiplied instantly.

That's why there were two of them. Identical twins. Identical to Trey Jr.

They'd fed from Tamara's corpse first, when there was still one of them inside the dead body of his son. Before he could grab a shovel and beat the tubes off his dead wife, the thing in Trey Jr. was two things. Just like that.

The next time they fed. When he brought a stray dog in the house, he stomped out the little wiggling things that pushed their way out of the twins' bodies as they fed.

That's when they're at their weakest. That's the *only* time they're weak. Just moments after they're…born?

* * * *

Treyvon takes the fire ax from the trunk and walks inside the funeral home.

Bob's dead. Mom and Dad are dead. Everyone's dead. Killed before they understood what was happening. Their bodies covered in sucker marks from where the tubes drained the panicked, grief stricken life from their bodies. The wounds dripped green.

The twins had followed the rules. Good boys.

They'd gone after the dead white woman first. Her corpse was Swiss cheese. The tubes entered through one hole, drank the precious death nectar from her veins, then existed through another before attacking the confused mourners.

In his mind's eye, Treyvon imagined her corpse lifting up out of the coffin, dancing like a marionette on wires. He imagined the shocked look on the family's faces as the movement caught their eyes. Their poor dead girl jittering around three feet above her coffin like she's being electrocuted.

Here, now, he looks at their dumbfounded corpses with a sneer and a smirk.

People parading in to see death, never expect it to touch them so soon. Their selfish grief. Their loved ones ripped from them so abruptly, so unfairly.

Not while I'm eating my TV dinner.

Not during my Oprah marathon.

They're blind to the danger. They fall like cattle.

They die easier than the stray dogs.

Treyvon steps over the dead bodies. The twins are in embalming fluid stasis. Wrapped in their hard shells. Even slowed down like this, Treyvon only has moments before the squirmy things solidify, take shape, and refuse to die.

He'd missed them when he made the closed casket mistake. When the twins didn't feed on the green stuff first.

When he'd lost the eye and hand.

Those squirmy things ended up in the funeral home's fire safe. Dragged down to the bottom of the ocean when Treyvon dumped them off the coast.

The last thing he'd heard as he tipped the safe off the side of the pier were the sounds of the little boys inside scratching the nails off their finger tips screaming, "No, daddy! Don't leave us! Don't let us die!"

They didn't die. They never die.

Maybe they fed on fish. Maybe they outgrew the safe and swam free. Multiplying. Eating giant squid and killer whales in schools of dozens of little Trey Jr.s. Their blue sacs and tubes trailing behind them, gobbling up shrimp and tuna.

He didn't care. He didn't care about any of it. Not anymore.

He was a custodian. A janitor. His job was to clean up Tamara's mess. His mess. Every third moon cycle.

Kill the people. Feed the twins. Kill the squirmers. Repeat.

For how long? What happened when age took him? The twins didn't age. They grew from those squirming things with the sacks and tubes outside their bodies into perfect copies of Trey Jr. and then stopped.

Twelve years on. They should be teenagers. They should be tall. Athletic. Like Treyvon's father. A basket ball player. Scholarships.

What happens when he lays down and quits? Who will stop them? Who will *know* how to stop them?

Treyvon swings the ax. The first twin's shell shatters. The squirmers are already digging out of Trey Jr.'s little face. He swings the ax again, breaking through the second twin's shell.

He stares at the squirmers coming out of the boys. He lets them thump out onto the hardwood floor of the funeral home.

He lets the ax fall from his hands.

He sits on the floor and he waits. Watches.

What happens when the squirmers take first blood? What happens when they grow Trey Jr.'s handsome face? What happens when every dark corner, every mountain peak, every deep ravine in the whole wide world is infested with his beautiful little man?

What happens?

Treyvon lights a cigarette and kicks a squirmer away from him. Its tubes are already growing, trying to suck the life out of the sole of his shoe. He takes a long drag from his smoke as half a dozen more squirmers fall out of the twins' faces.

He smiles at the growing legion of little Trey Jr.s.

"Let's find out." ▲

Princess or Warrior?
by S.W. Lauden

Mark checked his reflection in the liquor store window. The new clothes he had shoplifted earlier that day made for the perfect disguise. He held out his left forearm to check out his new tattoo. The pistol shoved into the stiff jeans was cold against his skin.

"Got any change?"

There was a different vagrant sitting on this stretch of sidewalk almost every night. Mark usually just ignored them, but this old man looked familiar. He flipped him a quarter and turned to leave. The coin skipped across the cement and rolled to a slow stop.

"Happy nineteenth birthday, *Marky*."

That was his mom's nickname for him. *And how did he know it's my birthday?*

"What'd you call me?"

"Take a seat, tough guy."

"No thanks, gramps. I gotta bounce."

"Knock it off with the street lingo. We both know you're a rich kid who's been to one too many rehabs."

"Who the fuck are you?"

"If I were you I'd be more worried about who those guys over there are."

Mark turned to look. Two middle-aged men were talking in the glow of a streetlight. Both were stocky and had trimmed mustaches.

"Are they cops?"

"Shut up and sit."

Mark dropped down beside him, trying to fight the creeping paranoia. He was starting to think that last blunt was a bad idea. The old man leaned in to study his bloodshot eyes. Mark thought to hold his breath, but there was no odor at all.

"Nice jumpsuit. You just escape from somewhere?"

"It's a long story. Where's the weed?"

"I, uh, smoked it."

"That explains why you can see me, but you're the only one. It must have been laced."

"With what?!"

"Nanophetamine. They're little microscopic robots that fry your synapses for an hour or so. Pretty good stuff, the first couple of times."

"Bullshit."

"Oh, it's real all right. One of the time troopers must have smuggled it back."

"*Time troopers?* Give me a break, dude. You must be more faded than I am."

"I know it's hard to believe, but I'll try to explain it. What I'm doing is called 'bouncing'. It's sort of like visiting your own memories. But the troopers? That's good old fashioned time travel."

"You're kinda freakin' me out."

"Show me your arm."

The old man leaned forward to study the puffy new ink. Mark waved his hand right through him.

"No way!"

"Keep your voice down. Is it Tuesday or Wednesday?"

"Wednesday."

"Christ. That explains it."

He was muttering to himself, but Mark tried to follow along.

"…I told that hacker exactly when to bounce me, down to the second. What a god damned rip off. I take it you haven't robbed the liquor store yet?"

"How do you know about that?"

"Oh, right. I should probably explain all of that. I'm you. You're me. Ta da."

He flashed a mostly toothless grin and shrugged.

"Come on, man. Get real."

"Fine. Let's get this over with. Ask me a question that only you know the answer to."

"What's my favorite color?"

"Blue."

"Favorite number."

"Eight. Give me something harder this time."

"What's my pet iguana's name?"

"Good old Fred. I really miss him."

"Damn. There's no way this is real."

"Suspicious is good, but we're running out of time. Tell me when I start flickering."

"Huh?"

"Your pupils aren't as big as they were. We probably only have a few minutes left."

"And then you just go back to wherever you came from?"

"No, I'll still be here for another couple of hours. You just won't be able to see me."

"Just get me some more nano-*whatever* then."

"I wouldn't, even if I could. Those little bastards can pile up until your skull starts bulging. I've seen heads explode on the transport ships. God awful mess."

"Man, I can't believe this. Tell me some more about what happens."

"Good news or bad news?"

"Good first."

"Ha. Why am I not surprised? Let's see—okay. You become a chemist."

"Really? I suck at science. But I can deal with that, I guess."

"Bad news is you get your degree in prison."

"Prison?!"

"What did you think would happen when you decided to start robbing liquor stores? Besides, prison is about the only place you can get a college degree after the collapse. Would have worked out perfectly if I was eligible for parole."

"Shit! You're flickering."

"Oh, before I forget."

The old man rolled up the sleeve of his jacket to reveal his own faded tattoo.

"This is one of the reasons I wanted to come back *yesterday*."

"Why?

"So you could pick a different tattoo. The guy at the parlor told me—*you*—it was the Chinese symbol for 'warrior', right?"

"Uh huh."

"I found out the hard way that it actually means 'princess'."

The old man watched carefully as recognition dawned across the boy's face.

"Don't tell me you went through all of this just to get the tattoo changed."

"I'm here about the liquor store. I just thought you should know what's coming."

"Oh."

"Listen to me. Things don't go exactly as you'd like them to tonight. The guy behind the counter has a gun too."

"Seriously? Does he shoot me?"

"He tries, but you fire first. 'Lucky shot' gets him right through the heart. That's how we ended up where I am right now."

"Prison."

"Yep. Life sentence."

"So you want me to skip the robbery…"

The old man was a fuzzy, fading image now. Mark tried to study his face, his eyes, his clothes. He didn't know if he would see him again, until he saw him in the mirror. His voice was fading in and out as he spoke his final words.

"No. We can't change things that much. Just don't shoot him. Everything will work out if you just don't pull your gun."

"Hey, wait! Doesn't that mean he'll shoot me?!"

"That way we can get the degree and get out in time to do something with it."

The old man sputtered and blinked until he was almost gone.

"Answer me!"

Mark stood up and checked his reflection in the window one more time. He looked over his shoulder to where the old man was sitting just a second ago. The gun was already in his trembling hand before he stepped inside the liquor store.

I am a warrior, no matter what my stupid tattoo says. ▲

Made in the USA
Middletown, DE
03 June 2016